THE AGENT'S
SECRET PAST

DEBBY GIUSTI

HARLEQUIN® LOVE INSPIRED® SUSPENSE

Recycling programs
for this product may
not exist in your area.

 LOVE INSPIRED BOOKS

ISBN-13: 978-0-373-44587-5

THE AGENT'S SECRET PAST

www.Harlequin.com

Printed in U.S.A.

Then he said to them all: "Whoever wants to be my disciple must deny themselves and take up their cross daily and follow me. For whoever wants to save their life will lose it, but whoever loses their life for me will save it."

—*Luke* 9:23–24

In Memory Of
Ginger Leary
A dear friend who loved books
and always encouraged me to keep writing.

PROLOGUE

Eight years earlier

The moon peered down between dark, billowing clouds and cast the Amish farmhouse in shadows. Rebecca Miller stepped from her car onto the one-lane, dirt road she knew so well and shivered in the frosty night air.

Leaving two years earlier had sealed her fate. She would not be welcomed nor accepted back unless—and until—she asked forgiveness. Something she could never do.

If only her father had believed her. Perhaps then, she would have remained in Harmony, Alabama, and spent the rest of her life wrapped in the familiar embrace of the Amish way.

Instead she had created a new future for herself in the military. Seemingly a drastic shift from the peace-loving community of her childhood, but then too many ignored what Rebecca knew so well. Evil existed even among the Amish.

After driving straight through from Fort Campbell, Kentucky, her legs were stiff and her shoulders tense.

Cautiously she climbed the front steps, her breath clouding the air. She shivered, anticipating her father's icy stare and quick rejection.

Her sister's words replayed in her memory. *I fear for my life.*

Rebecca tapped ever so lightly on the unlatched door. An even more chilling shiver snaked up her spine.

"Katie," she whispered, pushing the door open.

An acrid stench wafted past her before she saw her father

and the dark circle of blood pooling on the wooden floor beneath his chest. The cloying scent of copper clogged her throat and sent a jab of fear deep into her heart.

"Datt?" Without thought, she slipped back to her Amish past.

He lay on the hand-hewn floorboards his bearded face pale and drawn, life ebbing from his glassy eyes. Trying to assess which of the many stab wounds to stanch, Becca dropped to her knees and touched his outstretched hand.

Her father's eyes widened ever so slightly.

"Who was it?" she whispered, knowing even before he answered.

"Ja-Jacob," he stammered, ignoring the ban that forbid him from speaking to his daughter.

A shuffle sounded overhead.

Rebecca's breath hitched. "He's here?"

"Yah."

An unseen sword pierced her soul, the pain so intense she gasped for air. "Katie?"

He pointed to the pantry. "Go," he demanded, with a flick of his hand.

Recalling the times she and her younger sister had playfully hidden in the adjoining alcove, Becca hastened toward the pantry and inched the door open.

Her heart stopped.

Katie sat slumped against the wall, eyes open, face contorted in terror. Blood spilled from the gaping wound that sliced through her gut.

"No!" she moaned ever so softly.

Rebecca bit her fisted hand, unable to see anything except her sister's lifeless gaze. Guilt overwhelmed her. If she hadn't left, Katie would still be alive.

Footsteps sounded on the stairs and warned of his approach. Rebecca scurried back to the kitchen. Her father's head lay slack against his arm. She leaned down to touch his neck, feeling nothing except his soft flesh and prickly beard.

No pulse. No life.

A floorboard groaned on the landing. Close. Too close.

"Goodbye, *Datt*," she whispered.

Rebecca opened the door and slipped into the darkness. Once at her car, she glanced back.

Jacob appeared in the farmhouse doorway.

She could see the outline of his face, his beard, his lips snarling as he stared into the night.

"Who's there?" His eyes found her in the shadows.

He raised his fist in the air. "You cannot run from me, Rebecca. I will find you. When I do, you will die."

ONE

Eight years later

Run faster!

He was behind her, gaining speed.

The raspy pull of air in and out of his lungs grew louder, signaling his approach.

At any moment, she expected his work-worn hand to grab her shoulder and send her crashing onto the asphalt roadway.

How had he found her?

For the last eight years, she'd been stationed overseas. Three deployments to the Middle East, a twenty-four-month tour in Korea and a three-year assignment in Germany, all far from Harmony, Alabama, and her past.

She smelled his stench, an evil mix of hay and sweat.

"Becca," he whispered in her ear.

She gasped for air, woke from her nightmare, clawed at the sheets and blinked her eyes open, searching the darkness of her bachelor officer's quarters.

Sitting up in bed, she threw the covers aside and stepped onto the floor, the tiles cool to her bare feet. She shook her head in an attempt to scatter the dream that came too often.

She was at Fort Rickman, Georgia, not the Amish community where she had grown up.

Reality check. She had run away from Jacob Yoder eight years earlier. Supposedly he had died later that night after killing her father and sister.

Unnerved by the nightmare, Becca grabbed her holstered, service weapon off the nightstand and stumbled into the hallway on her way to the kitchen. She needed to hydrate her body and clear her mind. If only she could wash the memories away.

She placed the gun, which had been her almost constant companion for the last eight years, next to her purse on the kitchen table and opened the cabinet over the sink in search of a glass. A sickening smell, like rotten eggs, hit her full force.

Pinpricks of fear needled the nape of her neck.

She glanced at the gas cooking range. The burners were off. The flame on the pilot lights glowed crimson in the dark.

The smell was intense, overpowering, deadly.

Run!

She reached for her Glock and slipped her handbag over her shoulder as she raced through the living area to the back door. Fingers trembling, she fumbled at the lock, dead bolt and chain, her progress slowed by the protective safeguards she had put in place. For too long, she had tried to distance herself from Jacob, fearing he was still alive.

Her pulse pounded in her ear, like a ticking time bomb ready to explode. She had to escape before—

The door opened. She ran into the night, inhaling the pure, sweet air that filled her lungs.

In the distance beyond the common green space stood the older BOQ apartments. Even at this late hour a few lights glowed in the windows.

She glanced back at the newly built quad she'd moved into ten days earlier. The only occupant thus far.

Digging into her purse, she traded her gun for her cell and speed dialed the Criminal Investigation Division on post, where she worked. The noncommissioned officer on duty answered on the second ring.

"This is Special Agent Rebecca Miller. Notify the fire department and military police of a gas leak in the new BOQ quad on Eisenhower Drive. Tell them the only occupant has cleared the premises."

Before she could disconnect, the sound of unleashed fury rocked her world. The explosion lit the sky and mushroomed into a giant ball of fire.

The force of the blast pushed against her. She took a step back to keep her balance.

Her ears rang. Her eyes blurred.

She blinked against the brightness.

A surge of heat warmed her for an instant as it blew past, replaced with frigid winter air that penetrated her bones.

Jet-black smoke billowed from the windows of the bedroom where she had been asleep just moments earlier. The terrifying dream had saved her life.

Flames licked at the building's wood facade and devoured the decorative trim. "No," she gasped as the growing inferno turned night into day.

Sirens sounded in the distance. A trail of flashing lights signaled their approach. Fire trucks, followed by military police cars, raced into the parking area and screeched to a stop. Men in turnout gear spilled from the trucks. With swift, sure motions, they connected hoses to nearby hydrants and trained the heavy streams of water on the blaze while maintenance personnel hastened to cut off the gas supply that fueled the fire.

Footfalls pounded on the ground behind her. Becca turned at the sound, ready to defend herself again.

"Are you okay?" Colby Voss.

"How—how did you get here?" Instantly, she regretted the foolish question. No doubt, her fellow CID agent lived in the older BOQs on Sheridan Road, just across the open field.

"Are you hurt?" His eyes roamed her body as if searching for an injury or burn.

With her throat unexpectedly dry, she shook her head and raised her hand to reassure him. Her inability to find her voice caused an additional tangle of concern to wrap around her.

A pressure filled her chest. She clamped down on her jaw to ward off the wave of nausea that swirled around her. She didn't want to appear weak.

Especially not to a guy with inquiring eyes.

For the past eight years, no one had climbed her wall of defense. No one until Special Agent Colby Voss had sauntered into her cubicle ten days earlier to welcome her to Fort Rickman.

So much for maintaining her cool. Although right now she felt completely drained and unable to maintain anything, let alone her composure.

"What happened?" he asked, his eyes flicking between her and the firemen battling the blaze.

She wiped her hand across her forehead and pulled in another breath of cold night air. "I—I smelled gas. My stove was off. There must have been a leak someplace in the system."

"You were awake?"

A good question, but one she didn't want to answer. She had never told anyone about the reoccurring dreams.

"Just barely. I went into the kitchen for a glass of water and realized there was a leak."

"Good job getting outside."

She didn't need his praise or affirmation. Not tonight. Not when he was standing way too close and adding more anxiety to her already questionable stability.

Turning to stare at the raging inferno, she sucked in another mouthful of air and tried to calm her out-of-control pulse.

"It happened in the empty apartment next door," she said, convinced the gas had seeped into her kitchen from the neighboring unit. "Probably an accidental leak."

Had it been accidental?

Or was something else or someone else involved?

Her stomach tightened.

Surely not someone from her past.

* * *

Colby wanted to put his arm around Becca and quiet the fear that flashed from her eyes. He would have done exactly that, if not for the keep-out sign she wore around her heart, which he'd noticed the moment she reported for duty at CID Headquarters.

He had refused to be put off when they'd first met, especially since he had been the new CID agent two months earlier when he transferred from Fort Hood, Texas. He could read her body language and kept his welcome to a firm handshake and nod of his head, knowing all too well about self-sufficient women who didn't want or need a man in their lives.

Becca appeared to be a by-the-book type of agent who kept to herself. Not that he had been staring at her pretty face or green eyes with their flecks of gold. Eyes that she averted whenever he glanced her way.

That elusive shift of attention made him wonder if there wasn't something she wanted to hide. Perhaps he was reading more into what was only her nervous attempt to remain aloof, yet his gut feelings were usually right, and he kept thinking she had something buried beneath her neat and trim facade.

Two military police officers hustled toward them. Colby recognized the taller of the two as Gary Flanders, a put-together sergeant with an interest in joining the CID.

"Hey, sir, you know anything about what happened?"

Before Colby could answer, Becca drew in a deep breath and steeled her jaw with determination. "It was an explosion, Sergeant, in my BOQ."

Flanders pulled a notepad and mechanical pencil from his pocket while his partner stood to the side. "Can I get your name, ma'am?"

"Special Agent Becca Miller. I'm with the CID."

"You were the only resident in the new building?"

"That's correct. I arrived on post ten days ago and signed for the bottom apartment on the left. The one on the bottom right, as well as the two second-story apartments, were unoccupied."

"What happened?" the MP asked.

"I—I went into the kitchen for a glass of water and noticed a strong gas smell. Realizing the danger, I exited the building."

"Did you see anyone outside?"

She shook her head. "No one."

Wind blew across the clearing and ruffled the pages of the sergeant's notebook. He hunched his shoulders against the cold and glanced at her lightweight flannel pants and T-shirt. "The temperature's dropping, ma'am. Would you like to take shelter in one of the squad cars?"

"I'm fine, Sergeant."

Colby knew better.

Dressed as she was coupled with the plummeting temperature and the shock of seeing her BOQ in flames had to have an adverse effect on her. Even in the half-light, her face was noticeably pale and drawn.

He glanced down at her bare feet.

Time to make a command decision. "My BOQ is just across the clearing. We can continue to talk there."

He shrugged out of the thick fleece he'd grabbed on his way outside and slipped it over her shoulders.

She shook her head. "That's not necessary."

"Maybe not, but humor me."

Their eyes locked for a long moment.

Colby wanted to shake his head at her obstinacy. Someone needed to inform Ms. Miller that taking healthy measures to protect herself wasn't a sign of weakness.

What did she have to prove?

He took her arm.

She glanced down at his hand and then raised her gaze. "Really, I'm okay."

"Maybe, but the temperature is in the forties. You're not dressed for the cold. Neither am I."

He turned to the MP. "Sergeant, I'm in apartment 103, the first door on the left, should anyone need to question either Special Agent Miller or me."

"Yes, sir."

Colby motioned Becca forward and was somewhat surprised when she followed his lead. As tough as she had tried to be over the past few days, he had expected opposition. Not that he wasn't relieved.

Shock was a nasty complication that often went unnoticed. From the knit of her brow and the ever-so-slight slump to her usually ramrod-straight spine, Becca had been affected by the middle-of-the-night attack.

Who wouldn't be? To go from a near sleep to a race for your life could try the best of men—or women.

Glancing over his shoulder, he took in the seeming chaos as the on-post fire company worked to control the inferno that resisted their attempts at containment. The military police, post engineer, fire marshal and fire chief would survey the damage and photograph anything suspect. As much as Colby would have liked to check the property himself, someone needed to get Becca inside and out of the cold.

Tomorrow, the fire marshal and his entourage would sift through the rubble in hopes of uncovering the cause. More than likely, an accidental malfunction from a leak in a gas line or a faulty pilot light coupled with some type of spark.

At the far side of the grassy knoll Becca stopped and glanced over her shoulder at the blaze.

Colby heard the sharp intake of air as she shook her head.

"Was it Jacob?" she whispered.

He leaned closer, not sure if he had heard correctly.

"What did you say, Becca?"

Her eyes widened as if she had forgotten he was there.

So much for making a positive, first impression. Something his sisters would have teased him about mercilessly, if they found out.

Which they wouldn't.

"Did you say 'Jacob'?" he asked.

She shook her head. "I didn't say anything."

But she had. A man's name. Did she associate Jacob— whoever he was—with the explosion?

If so, Colby would keep watch in hopes she would eventually reveal more information. Maybe then he'd know what secrets she kept hidden behind her hauntingly hooded eyes and tantalizing reticence.

TWO

Becca hesitated for a moment before she stepped into Colby's BOQ and flicked her gaze over the leather couch and matching chair bathed in soft light from a floor lamp. A newspaper and stack of fitness magazines were arranged on the coffee table next to a collection of framed photos. She moved closer, her eyes drawn to a picture of a group of girls standing around a much younger Colby in uniform. The family resemblance couldn't be ignored.

"These must be your sisters?" she said.

"All five of them." She could hear the smile in his voice as he headed for the kitchen. "They insisted on a picture before I deployed to Afghanistan the first time."

A bittersweet moment for sure. Pride for their brother was tempered by the reality that he might not come home from war. Photos were something tangible to hold on to when all else was gone.

Graven images, the Amish called them. Her father had railed when she and Katie had come home with a snapshot a friend from town had taken of both of them. Her father had torn the picture into tiny pieces that Becca had tried to glue together later that night after he had gone to bed. If only she had that picture now. Instead, she had to rely on memories that faded with time.

"How do you take your coffee?" Colby called from the other room.

"With a little milk, if you've got it."

"Creamer okay?"

"Perfect."

A biography of General George S. Patton sat on a side table along with a number of training manuals. Military plaques and memorabilia hung on the wall next to citations for an army commendation medal, a meritorious service metal and two bronze stars. Impressive to say the least.

Not only was Colby good-looking but also competent, although she'd realized that the day they'd met. He'd been focused on business and not with making idle chitchat, for which she'd been grateful. Coming into a new unit was stressful. Having to keep up a flow of chatter made it even more so.

Turning, she noticed an open laptop on a desk in the corner. A plasma screen TV and two bookcases, stacked with three-ringed binders, filled the corner of the room and balanced the rather stark but comfortable furnishings. She approved of his uncluttered decorating style. Her own preference leaned to basic needs with few extras, which probably stemmed from her upbringing.

She accepted the coffee Colby offered and wrapped her hands around the mug, thankful for the warmth of the thick stoneware. After taking a sip, she gazed through the window at her own quarters visible in the distance. The once-sizable structure was now only a shell of steel support beams and charred debris.

Her hold baggage, containing the majority of her household items, wasn't due to arrive from Germany for another two weeks. The fire had destroyed only what she had brought in her luggage. All of which could be replaced.

"These might help." She turned to find Colby holding out a pair of heavy socks.

"Thank you." Accepting the offering, she quickly settled into a nearby chair and slipped the thick woolen coverings over her bare feet. "I didn't realize I was so cold."

"You were bordering on shock, which worried me."

"I appreciate your concern and the coffee." She smiled. Yet her attempt to remain upbeat was only halfhearted. The reality of what had happened tonight clamped down on her shoulders and wouldn't let go.

"Give me a minute to thaw out, then I'll head back to my BOQ," she told him.

"You won't be able to salvage anything tonight, Becca."

"Except the clothes that are still in my car." She laughed at her own foolishness. "I stopped at the commissary after work and lugged the groceries inside when I got home, but I failed to go back for the laundry I had picked up earlier. My gym bag's also in the trunk along with a pair of running shoes."

"What about your weapon?"

She ran her fingers over the purse still strapped to her shoulder. "I grabbed my Glock and purse before I ran. CID badge, military ID card, car keys. Everything I need is inside."

"Sounds as if you were expecting trouble."

Colby's comment struck too close to home.

When she didn't respond, he raised his brow expectantly.

Becca stood, needing to distance herself from his penetrating gaze. She walked into the kitchen and placed her mug in the sink.

"I'll drive you to your car," he said when she returned to the living room.

"Thanks, but I can walk."

"Not in this weather." He glanced at her feet. "I've got a pair of slippers that should fit you. They were a gift from my grandmother, but they're too small for me. The leather soles will protect your feet until you get the gym shoes from your car. You'll also need a jacket."

He disappeared down the hallway and returned with sweatpants and a hooded sweatshirt she pulled over her flannel pajamas. The slippers were roomy but warm.

"Maybe the fleece will be enough," she said, regarding the bulky coat he offered.

He shook his head. "You need more insulation if we're going to be outdoors for any length of time."

"What about you?"

"I'll wear my Gore-Tex. It's with my training gear in the back bedroom."

She shrugged into the jacket that smelled like sandalwood and lime and waited as Colby located his military outerwear and car keys.

Although she appreciated Colby's help, she needed to keep up her guard. No matter how nice or how good-looking he was, she didn't want anyone to complicate her life.

Her gaze returned to the window and the smoldering ruins beyond. Involuntarily, she shivered, regretting her youthful infatuation with Jacob Yoder when the Amish drifter had first stumbled into her life. How eagerly she had given her heart to him, not knowing he had taken up with an older woman—an infirmed Amish widow whose farm he coveted.

Bitter tears had stung Becca's eyes when she'd learned of their marriage. Even more difficult was her father's insistence that Becca help Jacob's sickly wife with housekeeping chores.

Jacob paid her father nicely for her services, and her needy *datt* turned a blind eye to what Jacob really wanted.

Her stomach soured, recalling when Jacob had lured her to the barn. She'd fought him off and narrowly escaped. Knowing her father would never believe her own innocence, she had run away from Jacob, her father and her Amish roots.

Two years later, her sister's phone call forced Becca to return home, but she arrived too late to save Katie or her *datt*.

With a heavy heart, Becca turned from the window, hoping to distance herself from the niggling concern that too often hovered close at hand.

Jacob was dead.

The case was closed.

But if that were true, then why did some inner voice keep warning her that Jacob Yoder was still alive?

Acrid smoke hung in the air around Becca's BOQ as Colby parked his green Chevy near her Honda and waited as she slipped on her shoes and shrugged off his suggestion to stay in the car. Worried though he was about her well-being, he admired her determination to get to the bottom of what had caused the explosion.

Together they crossed the street to where Sergeant Flanders stood next to his squad car.

"What's the latest?" Colby asked, raising his voice over the drone of the fire engines.

"We haven't been able to get close to the building, sir, but we've done a preliminary search of the surrounding wooded area and plan to retrace our steps after daylight. The post maintenance company has been called as well as the fire marshal, staff duty officer and post engineer. General Cameron was notified."

Becca stared over her shoulder at a second residence still under construction on the next street. "Has anyone searched the other building?"

"Not yet, ma'am."

She nodded to Colby. "Let's check it out."

Stopping at his car, Colby grabbed a Maglite from the trunk and handed a spare to Becca. "We might need these."

Flashlights in hand, they hustled across a narrow strip of green space and cautiously rounded the front of the structure. A utility van sat at the far end of the parking lot. The side panel decal read Peachtree Construction.

"Why would someone leave their truck in an isolated parking lot overnight?" Becca gave voice to what Colby was thinking.

"Time to have a look-see." He shone his flashlight

through the windshield. A ladder and tools were visible in the rear. An insulated coffee mug sat upfront in the console cup holder.

The doors were locked.

Becca raised her cell and relayed the Fulton County tag number to CID Headquarters. "Run the plates. Find out who the truck belongs to and get me an after-duty hours contact number for the company."

After disconnecting, she and Colby entered the second building through an open doorway. Their flashlights illuminated inner walls that were framed but lacked drywall.

Colby pointed to his left. "You go that way. I'll head right." Neither of them spoke as they made their way through the maze of two-by-fours. The only sounds within the building were their muffled footfalls on the concrete-slab floor and the wind that blew through the open doorway.

They met up at the far end of the structure. A rustle caused them to turn their lights on a rodent scurrying for shelter.

"That's one culprit we don't need to follow." Colby chuckled and then flexed his shoulders, hoping to ease the growing tension in his neck.

"I keep thinking that abandoned maintenance van might be important," Becca said as they exited the building and retraced their steps to the fire scene.

Sergeant Flanders looked up as they neared. "Find anything?"

"One of the construction vans," she said. "We're running the plates and getting a phone number for the company. Probably an Atlanta-based firm that landed the building contract."

"Any sign of the driver?" he asked.

Colby shook his head. "We searched the building. It's clean."

"Maybe the guy caught a ride home with a buddy."

The fire chief hustled toward them. He was tall with serious eyes that stared at them from under his helmet. "The fire's contained. I'll have some of my guys keep watch throughout the night. We don't want any hot embers to rekindle. One of my men is checking out something he saw in the unoccupied apartment on the bottom floor."

The chief's tone caused Colby's gut to tighten. He sensed the entire investigation was about to change.

A younger man in full turnout gear approached the chief. "There's a problem, sir. We found a body in the rubble."

Colby turned to look at Becca. This time she didn't avert her gaze. Instead she stared back at him.

"Was it Jacob?" she had whispered earlier.

Did the dead victim have anything to do with Becca?

"Hurry up and wait" was a standing joke in the army, although there was nothing funny about waiting for the medical examiner to arrive on site. After inspecting the body, he scheduled an autopsy for the following afternoon.

Crime-scene tape surrounded Becca's quarters. A name tag found on the victim identified him as the project manager for Peachtree Construction Company.

At this point, foul play couldn't be ruled out, but the most likely explanation was an accidental gas leak. Either the project manager had entered the unoccupied apartment suspecting a problem or had caused a malfunction once he was inside.

Becca kept thinking of what could have happened had she not awakened. Dark thoughts she had no reason to mention. Certainly not to Special Agent Voss, who hadn't left her side since the explosion.

His presence played havoc with her internal calm. She needed space and a few moments to compose her tired and confused mind. The reoccurring dream of running from

Jacob Yoder continued to haunt her. She sighed in an attempt to distance herself from the memory.

"Something wrong?" Colby asked.

Becca shook her head.

"You need some rest."

"I'm fine." A statement she had uttered too many times tonight. She wasn't used to having someone underfoot, although she did appreciate his concern.

"The chief reserved a room for you at the Lodge, Becca. It's time you headed there."

Special Agent in Charge Craig Wilson had arrived onsite shortly after Arnold's body had been uncovered. The CID commander now stood talking to the post provost marshal and Special Agents Jamison Steele and Brody Goodman.

Wilson was a tall African-American with broad shoulders and an innate ability to hone in on pertinent information that often solved a case. The high regard with which he was held in the entire CID was one of the reasons Becca had accepted the Georgia assignment. She could learn much under his direction.

Tonight she feared her credibility had been compromised. Wilson kept telling her to get out of the cold, yet he hadn't mentioned the temperature to Colby nor to the other CID personnel on scene.

Maybe it was the oversize coat she wore and the baggy sweatpants that made her seem needy. Something she never wanted to be.

Wilson slapped the provost marshal's back and nodded to Jamison and Brody before he walked purposefully toward where Becca stood.

"I've assigned Brody the lead on the death investigation."

She nodded. "Yes, sir."

"You were the only occupant of the BOQ, Becca. Any chance the explosion was targeted at you?"

"I'm not sure, sir."

"Has there been something in the past, a person who's given you trouble, someone who threatened to do you harm?"

"There was an incident in my youth, sir, but that person died some years ago."

Wilson rubbed his jaw. "It might be prudent to run down anyone you've arrested in the past few years, especially those who were incarcerated. Let's ensure you can account for anyone who might have a grudge to bear."

"Yes, sir."

The chief glanced at Colby. "Becca's new to post and doesn't know the surrounding area. Look into the explosion, Colby, and ensure it doesn't have anything to do with her past."

"I can handle it, sir," Becca objected.

Wilson's eyes narrowed. "Of course you can, but this might get personal. I want Colby to watch your back."

"But, sir—"

"Time for all of us to call it a night," Wilson said before she could state her objection. "The military police will guard the building. The crime-scene folks plan to go over the area as soon as the fire marshal gives them the okay. In spite of the investigation, General Cameron wants every available unit on post to participate in the half marathon tomorrow." He paused and stared at Colby. "You signed up to represent the CID?"

Colby nodded. "Yes, sir. Becca did, as well."

Wilson turned to her. "No need for you to run, if you don't feel up to it."

"I'm fine, sir."

"Then I'll see you both after the race."

As Wilson headed to his car, Colby touched Becca's arm. "There's nothing more we can do tonight. I'll drive you to the Lodge."

She shook her head, frustrated at being coddled by not

only Colby but also the chief. "Thanks, but I can drive myself. Besides I'll need my car in the morning."

The half marathon had been organized as a way to foster good relations between the town and military community, one of a series of events scheduled for the upcoming year that had the post commanding general's full support.

Colby smiled. "The least I can do is follow you home."

She shook her head. "Really, it's not necessary."

Either the tone of her voice or her narrowed gaze caused him to take a step back.

He raised his hands, palms out, and shrugged. "Of course, you're fine. I'll talk to you tomorrow."

Colby turned and headed to his car, leaving her standing in the parking lot. Hot tears burned her eyes, but she blinked them back and fisted her hands. For some reason, she hadn't wanted him to leave.

THREE

Only a little farther!

Becca pushed harder, her focus on the finish line. One more hill to climb to complete the 13.1K run, her first competition since she had arrived at Fort Rickman.

The cheers of the people lining the streets melded into a single roar that accompanied her up the incline. At the crest of the hill, she sucked air into her lungs, appreciating her body's response to the need for more oxygen.

The finish line lay fifty yards ahead.

Her time was good. Not good enough to win, but nothing to be ashamed of, either.

One last sprint. She kept her eyes on the goal. The Freemont running club official said something over the loudspeaker. Probably her number.

Her footfalls pounded the pavement.

Left, right, left, right...

Inhale, exhale. Inhale, exhale.

Everything faded into a blur.

Push. Harder. Faster.

She broke across the finish. Cheers erupted around her. Her body relaxed, and her pace slowed. She loped through a roped-off chute that would take her to one of the running club volunteers.

"Rebecca."

Someone from the sidelines called her name. A deep voice she knew too well. Fear tightened her spine.

She whipped her head to the right, the direction from which the voice had sounded, and stared into the crowd, searching for a face she would never forget. The face of a man—no, a monster—who had destroyed everything and everyone she had ever loved.

She scanned the bystanders—wives with babes in arms, parents and grandparents waving at their favorite runners, shopkeepers and community leaders supporting the town's first attempt to host the sporting event.

Surely her ears were playing tricks on her.

She would never forget the deep, almost soothing quality of his voice that persuaded even those most determined not to succumb to his diabolical charm.

Evil packed in a handsome face and muscular body.

Goose bumps pimpled her flesh. Despite the exertion, she shivered.

Someone shoved a plastic cup into her hand. "Water?" the guy asked.

She switched her gaze to the man and his outstretched hand. An older gentleman with kindly eyes.

Not Jacob.

"Great run," the man offering water enthused.

Nodding her appreciation, she took the cup and headed farther along the narrowing chute, still studying the crowd, unable to abandon her search.

She had heard Jacob's voice.

A high school volunteer checked the clipboard in his hand and marked off her number.

He pointed her toward the refreshment area. "Sports drinks are available at the table ahead. Burgers and dogs are on the grill when you feel like eating."

She downed the water, tossed the glass in a nearby trash receptacle and slipped through the crowd of those who had already finished the run.

"Good run." Another voice, one she also recognized.

She turned to see Colby approaching her, his angular face still flushed. His group had started ahead of hers.

"With so many runners, I didn't think I'd see you this

morning." His smile was warm, but his eyes were serious as if he were searching her face for some sign of weakness. He'd worn the same intense expression last night when he'd found her on the knoll immediately after the explosion.

"No reason to pass up a good race," she offered, hoping he wouldn't push for details.

"You were pretty worn out last night. You should have slept in."

She reached for another cup of water on a nearby table. "I could say the same for you."

He nodded. "You're right, but no reason to pass up a race."

She smiled in spite of herself. "You heard Chief Wilson last night," she offered as further reason for participating today. "He wanted everyone to support the event."

Once again, she flicked her gaze to the crowd. "Did you hear anything new from the fire marshal?"

"Only that he'll check the site this morning. The Atlanta construction company provided the name of the project manager. Ralph Arnold."

"The truck belonged to him?"

Colby nodded. "The Freemont chief of police asked for a court order to search the trailer he rented in town. They expect it to be signed by noon. I'll head that way later this morning"

"Give me the address. I'll meet you there."

"No reason to take two cars." He glanced at his watch. "I'll pick you up at the Lodge, say at eleven o'clock. We can stop by your old BOQ first and still arrive at Arnold's place ahead of the local police."

Glancing at her watch, she nodded. "That works for me."

Becca needed to buy a few items she'd lost in the fire, including a pair of flats to wear with the civilian clothes worn by the CID, instead of a military uniform.

Maybe Colby was right. She was pushing too hard, but it

was the only way she knew how to operate. Move forward. Don't look back. Don't think of what could have been. Don't allow anyone to get too close.

Then she glanced at Colby, seeing again that questioning lift of his brow. She would have to be extra careful to guard her past when he was around. For some reason, he seemed to sense the disquiet she carried in her heart.

After saying a quick goodbye, she turned toward the crowd, hoping her abruptness signaled her desire to be alone.

Coming back may have been a mistake.

Supposedly Jacob was dead and buried.

But Colby Voss was very much alive, and although the two men were polar opposites, they both posed a danger.

Jacob did because of the memories that tangled her dreams and impacted her life. Colby Voss was a danger in a completely different way, but she needed to guard against his charisma and his show of concern for her, just the same.

As she made her way through the crowd, her focus shifted back to Jacob.

He was dead.

She hoped.

Colby pulled to a stop at the red light, thinking of the warning signs that had flashed through his mind since he'd met Becca. If only she would lower her guard around him just a bit. Case in point, last night when she'd refused his offer to follow her to the Lodge.

Stubborn pride is what he called it, although not to her face. In truth, it was possibly her dislike of appearing weak or fear of revealing too much about herself. Now that Wilson had tasked them to investigate the explosion's tie-in with her past, Colby hoped to find a way to work with her and not against her.

Frustrated though he had been last night, he had hung back until she left the BOQ parking lot and had followed her to the Lodge. He'd made sure she arrived at the transient billets safe and sound and watched as she scurried inside. Lights came on in an upstairs room, and he'd seen her at the window before she closed the drapes.

Relieved to know she was safe, he'd driven home. Sleep had eluded him, and he'd spent a great portion of the night focused on Becca Miller and her determination to take care of herself.

Strong women were a challenge, to say the least.

He'd made that mistake once before and still carried the scars. Not physical, but painful nonetheless.

Foolish of him to have thought Ellen would change when they were both deployed in Afghanistan. Her independence and desire to go it alone had forced him to transfer to another forward operating base.

A mistake that haunted him still.

No matter how hard he worked to move on, the reality of what had happened was never far below the surface.

Meeting Becca had brought those memories to light again. Unresolved issues, his sister called them, but then she knew him too well. As much as he treasured their close sibling relationship, he didn't appreciate her uncanny ability to recognize his struggle.

Surely Becca Miller couldn't sense the undercurrent of his life. He prided himself on his outward control and on being a law enforcement officer who got the job done.

Turning into the lodge parking area this morning, he saw Becca standing in front of the building. She glanced impatiently at her watch.

He checked the dashboard clock. One minute past eleven. Did she think he was late?

Pulling to a stop, he reached across the passenger seat and opened the far door from the inside. Equal footing was what she wanted, which he would give her. Becca was a fellow army investigator. End of story.

So then why did he breathe in the flowery scent of her shampoo and take a second deep breath as if to ensure what he smelled was real and not his imagination?

He reached forward to help her click the seat belt in place. Their hands touched, sending a ripple of electricity up his arm. Nothing about Becca was his imagination. She was tall and slender, lean in a fit way but not too skinny, with a graceful neck and shoulder-length brown hair streaked with auburn.

She turned and greeted him, but his focus honed in on her green eyes, tired but bright.

"Did you get something to eat?" he asked.

"A couple power bars."

"You want some coffee. Maybe a burger at the drive-through?"

"Only if you do."

"I ate earlier at the race." Not that he couldn't eat again, but they were on a tight schedule, and he didn't want the Freemont police to arrive at the project manager's trailer ahead of them.

"Dental records should come in later today to officially ID Ralph Arnold's body," he told her as he pulled onto the main road and headed to her former BOQ.

"Have they contacted the next of kin?"

"A wife who lives in Marietta, just north of Atlanta. She talked to her husband yesterday evening. He was working late and had hoped to finish sometime before midnight and then drive home for the weekend."

"Now he's dead." Becca tsked. "I feel for the wife. Did they have kids?"

"Two boys."

"Growing up without a father will be tough."

Colby had to agree. "The question we need to answer is what was he doing in the vacant apartment?"

The fire marshal and two MPs were searching Becca's BOQ when they pulled into the quad parking lot.

"Find anything?" Colby asked after he and Becca had introduced themselves and flashed their identification.

"Nothing yet, but watch your step." The marshal pointed to the burned rubble covering the floor. "No way of telling if Mr. Arnold caused the problem or tried to fix what was amiss when he arrived."

"Wouldn't he have called in a gas leak and notified the fire department?" Colby asked.

"More than likely," the fire marshal said. "And if he'd used his cell when he was inside, a spark from his phone could have caused the explosion."

The marshal was a slender guy with bushy eyebrows. He glanced at Becca over the top of his glasses.

"After you smelled gas, Special Agent Miller, you told the MP last night that you exited through the rear of the building." He pursed his lips for a long moment. "Why didn't you use the front door?"

"My first thought was to get out. The back door was closer."

"Then you called CID Headquarters instead of 911?" the marshal pressed.

She nodded. "The number was programmed on my phone. I knew the person on duty could and would notify both the fire department and the military police immediately. Emergency operators ask questions that can delay the process."

The marshal raised his bushy brows. "We have an excellent emergency response system at Fort Rickman."

"That's good to know. I'll use it next time."

As if satisfied with her response, the marshal walked through the gaping hole between the two apartments and headed into the adjoining kitchen. Becca and Colby followed him into the living area of the unoccupied unit.

The stench of smoke and burned plastic hung in the air. Becca coughed to clear her lungs. Bending down, she brushed some debris aside.

Colby edged closer. "What did you find?"

"Glass shards."

"An overhead light fixture perhaps," he mused.

"Maybe, but most lights are opaque or frosted." She glanced at an opening in the nearby wall. "Guess what used to be here?"

Colby stepped back to view the entire room and realized where she was headed. "The front door."

"That's right. Flanked by panes of clear glass."

Colby knew the significance of finding the glass within the house. "If the panes had blown with the explosion, the shards would be outside the footprint of the structure."

"But they're inside," she said, her face drawn. "The shattered glass makes me think someone else was in the apartment. Someone who had broken one of the glass panes to gain entry into the apartment before the explosion."

"Ralph Arnold had a key to the unit." Colby glanced again at where the front door had been. "If Arnold noticed the broken window, he may have entered the unit to determine what had happened and inadvertently surprised the intruder."

"And was killed for that reason," Becca added. "Then the perpetrator turned on the gas. The explosion covered up any evidence he left behind."

"Evidence and a dead body. But if that's the case, then why was the perpetrator here in the first place?"

Becca didn't want to share her suspicions with Colby. She wasn't ready to discuss her past and the man she had run from years ago.

Had Jacob Yoder found her? If so, he'd entered the vacant apartment earlier in the day and had holed up until she came home from work and eventually headed to bed.

The project manager had surprised Jacob, but Arnold wasn't the target of last night's explosion.

Becca was.

FOUR

Becca was eager to find something—anything—to refute her theory about being the target of last night's explosion. If only she could uncover incriminating evidence in the project manager's trailer that would point to his involvement in an illegal operation. Drug smuggling, embezzlement, even human trafficking. Bottom line, she needed a motive for his death that would draw attention away from her.

She and Colby arrived at the trailer and were joined by two officers from the Freemont Police Department. Wearing vinyl gloves, they searched all the logical places where a perpetrator would hide anything he didn't want the police to find.

When their search proved futile, Becca turned to more ingenious hiding spots, but even then she found nothing that seemed questionable.

If she couldn't uncover evidence relevant to a crime, her initial assumption about Jacob Yoder being alive might prove true, which made her even more determined to keep looking.

After searching Arnold's bedroom, she pounded her fist against the wall.

"Take it easy, Becca," Colby cautioned from the hallway.

Undeterred by his comment, she tapped again. "Hear that hollow sound? It could be a secret hiding compartment."

Brody ran his fingers over the walls and stood close enough for her to notice his aftershave. She took a step back, needing to keep her focus on the search instead of his strong hands and the heady scent that wafted around her.

Eventually, he shook his head. "The wall's secure. No cubby holes. No secret hiding spots. Let's keep looking."

He was right, of course, yet she was frustrated by the

fruitless search as well as her less than professional response to Colby's nearness. She moved into the living area, forcing her thoughts back to the case. Nothing could be ruled out at his point, but even the idea of a drug deal gone south seemed remote.

The trailer had been in pristine condition when they first arrived. Neat and tidy with a number of scrapbooks containing pictures of Mr. Arnold receiving awards from his superiors. Religious books were stacked on the coffee table, as well as a scattering of pictures of his wife and kids, all of which indicated that he was a salt-of-the-earth type of guy. A well-worn Bible lay on the couch as if he'd read scripture before he had left for work.

More than likely, Arnold's death was a wrong-place, wrong-time incident. Making his rounds last night, he had seen the broken windowpane and entered the BOQ to check it out, never expecting the perpetrator to be inside. Instead he should have called the military police on post and asked them to investigate.

As Colby drove them back to post, Becca kept her eyes on the road ahead instead of on him. She was becoming much too interested in Colby, and instead, she needed to come up with a logical reason for the initial break-in. She quickly narrowed it down to two options. Either the killer entered the empty BOQ because he wanted a place to hole up overnight, or he was there to do her harm.

"You're quiet." Colby broke the silence. "Want to share what you're thinking?"

Exactly what she didn't want to do.

She tried to act nonchalant. "Just wondering about the killer."

"Anyone giving you a hard time recently?" He flicked a sideways glance her way. "We make enemies in this business. Wilson said as much last night. Is there someone who has a beef with you? Someone you sent to prison and now he's out? Even an old boyfriend who wasn't happy when you dumped him?"

"No old boyfriend."

Colby nodded as if relieved, which made her smile.

"That's one down," he said. "Anyone grumbling about being set up or complaining you pushed too hard?"

"Probably everyone I've arrested."

"Do you remember anyone who was more vocal than the rest, more agitated, more out to seek revenge?"

She shook her head. "No one comes to mind."

"You're sure?"

"Yes, I'm sure." She straightened her skirt, still frustrated with her own response to his nearness. "You sound as if I'm under interrogation."

"Of course not. It's just—" He tapped the steering wheel. "I get this feeling you're holding something back. Is there anything you're not telling me that might have relevance to this investigation?"

If only she could tell him about Jacob, but an investigation depended on facts and not some pie-in-the-sky suspicion that a buried killer could come back to life.

Becca had worked hard to get to this point in her career and still walked a tight rope to fit in with a predominantly male work group. She didn't need to spout nonsensical supposition.

"As we both know," she offered, hoping it would ease the tension between them. "The simplest explanation is often the one that proves true. The guy who broke in probably needed a place to hole up overnight. He could have been cold and tried to light the stove to keep warm. If the pilot light was out, the gas could have filled the apartment and caused the explosion."

Colby glanced at her. "And this homeless guy seeks refuge on an army post complete with gate checks and 24/7 security?"

"I admit it doesn't sound likely." He was right. Security was tight on Fort Rickman. If the project manager hadn't seen the broken window, the military police would have.

"You want to hear my theory?" he asked.

She licked her lips, not knowing what to expect. "Okay."

"The perp was interested in you, Becca."

She held up her hand. "That's ridiculous."

"I beg to differ. It's the most plausible explanation." He hesitated and then added, "Anything in your past that could play into the explosion?"

He wouldn't let up, and she couldn't chance what would happen if he knew the truth. "Not that I know of."

"You were fearful last night when the fire was raging, and when we were walking to my BOQ you mentioned some guy's name."

"I don't remember saying anything specific. Besides, my new home was going up in flames. It wasn't that I was fearful, Colby. I was relieved to have gotten out alive."

He nodded. "My oldest sister—her name's Gloria—claims I survived Afghanistan because of her prayers and God's mercy. He must have been watching over you last night."

Thoughts of her own sister made her eyes burn with unexpected tears. She turned her gaze to the side window, not wanting Colby to notice.

His hand reached for hers. "Did I say something wrong?"

For a guy, he had a keen knack of sensing her emotional struggle. Plus, his touch was reassuring, yet she didn't want to seem like an emotional female. In truth, a lot had happened and if she added fatigue to the mix, she could almost forgive herself for appearing weak.

"My...my sister died eight years ago. I keep thinking I've worked through my grief, then something happens and it rushes back again."

"Look, I'm sorry. I didn't mean to make you cry."

"You didn't do anything wrong, and I'm glad Gloria prayed for you." She offered him a weak smile, hoping her face wasn't blotched and her nose beet red from the tears.

"My father always said I was headstrong, but my sister Katie claimed I just needed prayer to keep me in line. In hindsight, it was probably wanderlust that got me in trouble at home and made the military seem a natural way of life."

"You transferred to Fort Rickman from Germany?"

She nodded, relieved the conversation had moved to neutral ground. "I asked to work for Chief Wilson. There was an opening, and I got my first choice of assignments."

"Which means your record is excellent or you wouldn't have been selected for the job."

"Maybe it was my sister's prayers finally coming to fruition."

He smiled and squeezed her hand again, a reassuring gesture, she told herself, that any friend would offer.

They rode in silence for a few minutes before he asked, "Did you meet Dawson Timmons when he stopped by the office last week?"

She remembered both him and his wife. "Nice guy. His wife Lillie was equally so. They invited me to the barbecue at his farm."

"Just about everyone in CID Headquarters will be there."

"It was kind of them to include me."

"They're good folks. I served with Dawson at Fort Hood. He transferred here and met Lillie. Now he's out of the army, owns a farm and is living the good life."

"A soldier turned farmer." Becca smiled. "His wife must have changed his mind about law enforcement."

"Actually, he claims to love working the soil." Colby thought for a moment before asking, "Why don't I pick you up tomorrow? We can drive there together. That way you won't have to worry about getting directions."

"Dawson drew a map for me when he was in the office. Between that and my GPS, it shouldn't be difficult to find."

"Call me if you change your mind."

Becca didn't believe in mixing business with her social life. No reason to give folks anything to talk about, especially when she already seemed much too affected by the special agent.

The Lodge appeared on the left. Colby turned into the parking lot. "Did you get the memo about Monday and Tuesday being training holidays?"

"I did." Becca opened the passenger door and stepped onto the sidewalk. "We'll probably be working on the investigation both days. Thanks for the ride."

She waved goodbye and waited until Colby drove away before she dug in her purse for her phone and hurried to her car. Once behind the wheel, she called the former sheriff in Harmony, Alabama.

"McDougal," a raspy voice answered.

"Sir, you may not remember me. I grew up in the Amish community. Now I'm with the Criminal Investigation Division at Fort Rickman, Georgia. There's been a crime on post that may be related to my father and sister's murders."

"Rebecca Mueller, is that you?"

"Yes, sir. Although I go by Becca Miller now."

"What can I do for you?"

"I'm driving to Harmony this afternoon and should be there in a couple hours. I'd like to talk to you about the case."

"I retired and don't have access to any of the old files, although I'd be happy to see you."

She glanced at her watch. "I need to stop by Elizabeth Konig's house first. It might be late afternoon before I get to your place."

"Do you mind telling me what you want to discuss?"

"Whether Jacob Yoder could still be alive."

* * *

Colby left the Lodge parking area and turned onto the main road irritated with himself. Once again, he thought of Becca's flushed cheeks and eyes brimming with tears. Grief was insidious, like a sly fox that doesn't want to be seen, until something flushes the animal into the open. His sister had a way of bringing his own pain to light by often saying the one thing that reminded him too much of Ellen.

Death was so…

He hunted for the right word.

Final.

He'd learned that the hard way. Evidently, Becca still had more to learn. From now on, he'd try to be more sensitive to her feelings.

At least, they'd talked openly about her security. Colby planned to keep revisiting the subject until he was convinced she realized the danger she might be in.

A good CID agent had a list of enemies. Becca was no different. Yet she hadn't been forthright about any investigation or arrests that ended badly. Call it his sixth sense, but he distinctly felt she was holding something back.

Jacob? He had heard her mention the name last night, yet she'd denied it.

While searching the trailer today, she'd been like a coon dog hot on the prey's trail. Only they had uncovered nothing of interest, not even a shred of evidence that would raise suspicion. Brody Goodman, one of the other special agents, had checked into Arnold's past. The man's record was lilywhite. No arrests. No trouble with the law. Not even a traffic violation. He served as a deacon in his church and was voted favorite coach of his son's Little League.

Yet Becca had insisted if they looked long enough, something would be uncovered, and when they returned to post empty-handed, she'd seemed withdrawn and mildly agitated. Perhaps she had hoped Arnold would be found culpable to take the heat off her. The project manager might have stumbled upon the perp, but Arnold wasn't the reason the guy had been hiding in the BOQ in the first place. Seemed logical that he'd been there because of Becca. Which Colby had mentioned, and she had tried to refute.

He pulled to a stop at an intersection and thought back to her clipped speech and guarded eyes. Becca was an unknown entity. She had transferred from an overseas assignment and had never served previously with any of the Fort Rickman special agents. As much as Colby wanted to believe she was competent, she could be involved in something suspect.

The light changed. He picked up his cell and tapped in the number for CID Headquarters. Sergeant Raynard Otis answered. "Ray, put me through to the boss."

Once Wilson came on the line, Colby filled him in on the clean search of Arnold's trailer. "Sir, I'm concerned Special Agent Miller may have been the targeted victim of the explosion as you mentioned last night."

"Have you discussed your suspicions with her?"

"She's quick to discard the idea, which makes me concerned about her personal safety."

"I wanted her to work with you, Colby. Is that a problem?"

"Ah, no, sir."

"I realize this puts you in a difficult position. Especially if she's unwilling to realize she might be in danger. Keep tabs on her as best you can until we have a better picture of what happened last night. From the short time she's been with us, it's evident she guards her privacy. Make sure her self-sufficiency doesn't get her into trouble. Do you understand what I'm saying?"

"Yes, sir."

Colby disconnected and made a U-turn when the light changed. Wilson was right. He'd put Colby in a difficult position. Keep Becca safe when Becca didn't think she was in danger. Worse than that, she probably didn't want him around.

Approaching the Lodge, he noticed her silver Honda turn out of the parking lot, heading toward the main gate. Could be a long day if she was like his sisters and planned to spend time shopping.

Colby hadn't expected to play bodyguard to another CID agent. A waste of taxpayer money, in his opinion, but Wilson was in charge so he would comply.

Just so Becca didn't spot the tail.

Leaving post, she increased her speed and took a road that bypassed Freemont. He glanced down at his gas gauge relieved that he'd filled up at the Post Exchange gas station two days ago. Settling into his seat, he hung back a number of car lengths and accelerated to keep up with her. At the speed she was driving, Becca seemed determined to get somewhere fast.

Maybe she wasn't heading for the mall after all.

Colby programmed a selection of music CDs that filled the Chevy with country songs about lost loves and broken hearts. He sang along and tapped his hand against the steering wheel in time to the music.

Becca seemed oblivious to his tail, which concerned him. She should have been more observant. Wilson had been right. She needed someone to watch her back. Colby planned to do exactly that.

Nearly two hours passed before she slowed her speed. A road sign welcomed them to Harmony, Alabama. Becca drove to the center of town, turned onto a side road and braked to a stop in front of a small one-story ranch.

Colby pulled to the curb in front of a neighbor's house on the opposite side of the street. Turning off the ignition, he scooted down in the seat and watched Becca scurry along the sidewalk to the modest home. She glanced over her shoulder before she knocked.

He slumped down farther. The last thing Colby wanted was for Becca to realize she was under surveillance.

FIVE

Memories of riding to town in her *datt's* buggy flooded over Becca as she stood on Elizabeth Konig's front porch. The locals were used to the Amish way, but visitors and tourists, who came to town specifically to see the plain folks, frequently pointed and stared. Even at a very young age, Becca knew the Amish were different from the *English*.

In summer, she and her sister would romp barefoot through the tall grass and giggle at night when their father thought they were asleep. Instead they whiled away the hours, talking about their dreams for the future. Katie had wanted to marry and raise a family. Becca's aspirations included world travel. Too often, her dreams leapfrogged from one destination to another, each far beyond anything an Amish girl from Harmony could ever hope to experience.

Now, wrapped in the warmth of those bygone moments, Becca knocked on the front door and glanced beyond the well-manicured lawn to the grove of tall pecan trees that surrounded the property. A thick stand of pines clustered beyond the pecan grove and provided privacy, in spite of the in-town location.

Twenty years older than Becca, Elizabeth Konig had wanted more to life than staying on her father's farm or marrying one of the local Amish boys. She and Becca had that in common.

As a young woman, Elizabeth had left the Amish community and had taken a job in a local fabric store in town. An expert with needle and thread, she was soon teaching classes and making extra money with her sewing. She rented a small apartment in the basement of the shop where she worked and eventually inherited both the store and the owner's nearby home when her spinster boss passed away.

Not only was Elizabeth an accomplished seamstress, but she was also a gifted student and went on to graduate college by taking night classes.

Typically, Amish education ended at the eighth grade, but Becca's mother wanted more for her girls. Her dying wish had been for Elizabeth to homeschool her daughters. To his credit and out of deference to his deceased wife, her father had allowed Becca and Katie to continue their studies, and each girl had eventually earned her high school diploma.

When Becca had run away from Jacob the first time, she turned to Elizabeth for support. A friend as well as teacher, Elizabeth had driven Becca to the recruiting office in a neighboring town and had supported her decision to join the military, which had provided not only a livelihood but also a way for Becca to leave Harmony.

Three years later, Katie had called Becca from the seamstress's house. After her sister's murder, Becca had run back to Elizabeth. With the older woman's encouragement and support, Becca had notified the sheriff of the horrendous slaughter that had occurred at the Mueller farm, and Elizabeth had stayed with Becca during the interrogations that ensued.

Filled with gratitude for the pivotal role Elizabeth had played in her life, Becca smiled when she heard her dear friend's lyrical voice from inside the house.

A sense of homecoming stirred deep within Becca, and tears filled her eyes when the door opened.

"Oh, Rebecca, you've come home."

"Yah, Elizabeth. *Webishtew?* How are you?"

"Better now that you are here." The older woman wrapped her in a heartfelt embrace filled with love and welcome.

"You have grown even more beautiful." The older woman's eyes were damp when she pulled back to stare at Becca.

"You make me blush, Elizabeth."

"It is not prideful if I say it, Becca. Now come in," she insisted, opening the door even wider. "I just made a pot of tea. You must tell me what you are doing in Harmony."

The small living room and adjoining dining area were as meticulously cared for as when Becca had been there eight years earlier.

"Your store is doing well?" she asked as Elizabeth poured the tea.

"Well enough that I have ladies who help me. I usually go in twice a week to catch up."

"And you're happy?" Becca accepted the cup Elizabeth offered.

"Is that the question that troubles you after all these years?"

"There are other things I want to discuss, but first let's enjoy our tea."

The older woman placed the sugar bowl and spoon on the table in front of Becca. She relaxed in a chintz-covered chair, feeling at peace in the familiar surroundings. Even Elizabeth's motherly scrutiny brought comfort.

The older woman arranged a large slice of homemade pound cake on a delicate China plate and topped it with strawberry preserves. "Eat. You are too thin."

Becca laughed as she accepted the cake, enjoying the rich buttery taste mixed with the tart berries. As the two women sipped their tea, Becca shared highlights of her overseas journey before she got to the reason for her visit.

"I'm sorry I didn't write, Elizabeth. When I left after Katie and *Datt* died, I…I needed to leave everything behind."

Elizabeth took a sip from her cup. "You were running away from your past, but you are back now. That's what matters."

"Also…" Becca had to be careful how she broached the

subject. "I was worried about your safety. I feared my letters could put you in danger."

"But how could that be?"

"Have you heard anything of Jacob Yoder?"

Elizabeth's eyes widened. "Why would I? He died years ago as you know."

"I believe the sheriff may have been wrong in identifying the body as Jacob's."

The older woman made a clucking sound as she patted Becca's hand. "You were never satisfied with life as it was and always searched for something more. You must accept what Chief McDougal told you and not fear the past."

"I survived what happened, Elizabeth. The past has no hold on me. What I fear is that Jacob is alive." Becca explained about the explosion and hearing his all-too-familiar voice at the Freemont race.

"Accidents happen even with modern gas appliances," Elizabeth insisted. "And surely the voice you heard belonged to someone else."

Becca had hoped Elizabeth would side with her, but inwardly, she knew her theory about the burial mix-up was hard to grasp, even for such a dear friend.

"I'm going to talk to those who live near the Yoder farm," Becca said. "Someone might have information."

"They will not be open with their welcome."

"I know that all too well." Becca had left the community and severed ties with her past. She would not be accepted back unless she repented and asked forgiveness for leaving the Amish way of life. Neither of which she planned to do.

After finishing the tea, Becca stood and hugged her friend once again. "There are so few people with whom I can openly talk about the past, Elizabeth. Thank you for listening."

"You are like family, Becca. Come back often."

Outside, the winter sun hung low in the sky. Becca raised

her hand to shield the glare from her eyes. With her gaze averted, she almost ran headfirst into someone leaning against her car.

Looking up, she gasped. "Colby?"

A swirl of emotion rose up within her. Confusion. Frustration. Anger. "What are you doing here?" she demanded.

She glanced around and spied his car parked across the street on the next block. Her eyes widened. "You followed me here."

"I wanted to help," he offered.

She squared her shoulders and shoved her jaw forward with determination. "I don't need your help, if it includes secrecy and duplicity."

"What you need is to realize you're in danger," he countered, sounding as frustrated as she felt. "Traipsing all over the countryside isn't smart, especially if someone's after you. You didn't know I was behind you because you were so focused on driving here that you failed to notice my tail. That means someone wishing to do you harm could have followed you, as well."

She stared at him, weighing what he had just said. Her anger dissipated somewhat as she realized he was right. Had she been so centered on seeing Elizabeth that she hadn't thought of her own personal safety?

Silence settled between them for a long moment before Colby asked, "Do you mind shedding a little light on why you're here?"

When she didn't respond, he stepped closer. "Come on, Becca. We're both interested in finding out what happened on post. What aren't you telling me that might have bearing on the explosion and murder?"

She shook her head, still not willing to reveal anything to Colby. "My past doesn't play into the investigation."

"You're parsing words."

Which she was, but she didn't know if she could trust

him. She never talked about growing up Amish to anyone in the military. Not that she told untruths. Rather, she provided information only on a need-to-know basis.

Becca stared into his eyes, expecting agitation or anger. Instead she was touched by the depth of concern and strength of compassion she saw.

Confrontation would be easier to handle.

Jacob Yoder scared her, but being defenseless around Colby Voss scared her, as well.

"When do you plan to drive back to Fort Rickman?" Colby asked, hoping she would reply at least to that one question.

She dropped her hands. Her guard seemed to slip at the same time.

"Later this evening," she said, all the while trying to step around him.

He moved in front of her, blocking her way.

"Colby, please."

"Please what, Becca? Please don't interfere? We've had a murder on post, and the killer may have been stalking you. I need answers to questions you aren't willing to talk about, like what he was doing in the quadruplex last night, and why you came here and what you hoped to find. I thought we were working together."

She stared at him long and hard as if determined to elude his questions, yet he wouldn't be brushed aside.

Nor would he stop staring into her pretty but confused green eyes. She eventually blinked, which seemed to open the dam that had held her in check. Her lips quivered. She wrapped her arms around her waist and blinked back tears that made him want to reach for her.

"My sister was murdered eight years ago. So was my father." The words tumbled out as if of their own volition.

Colby kept his expression passive. Inside he felt like she'd punched him in the gut. He hadn't seen that coming.

"Jacob Yoder, the man who killed them, died in a house fire that same night." Becca spoke rapidly as if she needed to pour out the information before she had second thoughts. "His wife also succumbed to the blaze. The local sheriff called it a murder-suicide and closed the case."

"Which you thought needed to remain open?"

"I'm not sure the body they found in the burned rubble was the killer's."

Colby didn't want to stop the flow of information or deflate her determination of getting at the truth, but chances were good that the body was who the old sheriff said it was. Errors happened, but logic made him wonder if Becca was digging up something that had been buried for a reason.

"What about dental records?" he asked, hoping to gently expose the fallacy in her supposition.

She shook her head. "None were available."

"DNA?"

"It wasn't done."

"An autopsy?"

"Both bodies were buried without a medical examination."

Becca bit her lower lip and stared at him intently. She was waiting for a response. He didn't want to provide false hope at this point and decided posing another question might be the safest tactic.

"If the body wasn't that of the killer, whose was it, Becca?"

"That's what I need to determine and why I plan to talk to Jacob's neighbors."

Colby glanced at the row of small homes lining the quiet residential street. "Townspeople who live nearby?"

"Folks from the country."

Horses' hooves clip-clopped over the pavement. Becca

turned at the sound. A young girl, not more than twelve or thirteen sat in the seat of a buggy next to an older bearded man.

"There's something you need to know." Becca pointed to the Amish lass. "That young girl? When I look at her, I see myself. In those days, I was Rebecca Mueller. I lived on a farm with my father and sister Katie. I rode in a buggy, Colby, because I grew up Amish."

Becca couldn't stop talking.

For too many years, she had bottled up the past and ignored her early life. Now that she had revealed the truth to Colby, she wanted him to understand the way her life had been.

Colby took her arm and hurried her along the sidewalk toward where he had parked his car. All the while, she continued to fill him in on her father and sister, their farm, their poverty. She stopped when he opened the passenger door.

"Get in, Becca. If you're determined to visit Jacob's neighbors, then I'm driving. I don't want you on some back road all by yourself. Especially if Jacob is alive. We'll return for your car later."

A sense of relief swept over her. "Then you believe me?"

"I don't know what to believe at this point. But I know you see a connection between what happened to your family and the explosion at Fort Rickman. We're working together so I'm in this with you."

At least Colby was being honest, which she appreciated. Plus, he was willing to consider her theory about Jacob. Having a second investigator reviewing her father and sister's deaths as well as the farmhouse fire that had claimed two lives would be beneficial. Maybe Colby would pick up something she had overlooked.

Something else took hold as Becca directed him out of town and along a narrow road that headed into the country.

A sense of connection. She had been alone for so long. Having Colby at her side meant she could share the workload as well as the anxiousness that frequently welled up within her when she dealt with a death case.

Her father had talked about his own anxiety after her mother had died. Too often he grumbled at having no one with whom to share the load, the work, the worry about the farm or what he often referred to as his *cross.* Simon of Cyrene had helped Christ, her father had frequently groused, but he had no one.

Becca had been hard-pressed to find a comparison between her father's situation and the Lord's, yet she couldn't escape the sense of guilt he seemed willing to place on her shoulders. The guilt of her not doing enough or being strong enough or being born the wrong gender had turned into a constant litany around the Mueller house.

Now that she had shared some of her past with Colby, that crush of guilt eased. He was a good man with a finely honed sense of right and wrong and a desire to keep her safe, which she appreciated.

Becca had never wanted a man's protection, no doubt due to her own history with her father and Jacob. She'd always taken care of herself, but ever since she'd met Colby, she'd felt an inner tug to give up some of her insistence on control.

At times, the feeling scared her, but at the moment, she was overcome with relief.

"Will the neighbors want to talk?" Colby asked as they drove into the country.

"I'm not sure. They'll remember I left them eight years ago, in spite of what happened to my father and sister."

Cresting a hill, a patchwork of farms appeared in the distance along with a line of cars that passed them as they headed deeper into Amish country.

"Things have changed," Becca said as a minivan and two

four-door sedans sped past. "This area used to be peaceful and isolated. Looks like tourists enamored with the plain life are flocking here now."

Colby hadn't expected traffic this far from town.

"What happened to your family's place?" he asked.

"I've held on to it. The house isn't much and the little bit of land my father owned was unproductive. A local developer was interested in buying the property, but I was getting ready to deploy and never replied to his request."

Becca pointed to the upcoming intersection.

"Turn right at the next road and stop at the first farmhouse. The Hershberger property adjoins Yoder's farm. Sarah Hershberger was an old friend. I'm hoping she'll talk to me today."

A woman stood at the side of the two-story structure, hanging laundry on a clothesline. Seeing the car pull into her drive, she scurried toward her house as if eager to get inside.

Becca called to her as she and Colby stepped from the car. The Amish woman was as tall as Becca and pretty in a homespun way with her long dress, apron and bonnet. She glanced at Colby with some sense of hesitancy as Becca motioned him forward.

Once Becca had made the introductions, Sarah flicked her gaze to the nearby road and motioned them toward her home. "You must come inside. I'm not sure who might be watching."

"You're worried?" he asked.

"It would be better if others don't see me talking to Rebecca. She left the community and turned her back on the Amish way. I accepted her decision. Some do not."

Yet, Sarah was ushering them into her house.

The main room was large with a long, hardwood table and benches that appeared hand hewn.

She pulled the curtains closed before she pointed to the table. "Sit. Please. Do you wish something to drink?"

Becca held up her hand. "We just need to ask you a few questions."

Sarah tugged at the edge of her apron and scooted onto the bench across from them. "What is it you need to know?"

"Jacob Yoder," Becca said.

Sarah studied her friend with serious eyes. "What are you asking, Rebecca?"

"I'm asking if you've seen him."

"The sheriff would know. You should talk to him."

"He'll tell me Jacob is dead," Becca insisted. "I need the truth."

"The truth is not always easy to tell." Sarah licked her lips. "The day before your father and Katie were killed… The day before the Yoder house burned, someone knocked at our door."

"Go on," Becca encouraged.

Colby's pulse kicked up a notch, realizing the importance of what she was about to share.

"A man asked for Jacob," Sarah continued. "I told him he had the wrong house. He said he was Ezekiel Yoder. Jacob's brother."

Colby leaned closer. "Did you see Ezekiel after the fire?"

"No."

"You're sure it was Jacob's brother?"

"That's who he said he was. I would not make this up."

"Of course not." Becca patted her old friend's hand and kept her voice neutral. "Did anyone else know about Jacob's brother?"

The Amish woman shrugged. "I do not know. No one has mentioned him."

"What about Jacob?" Colby asked.

Sarah wiped her hand across the smooth surface of the polished table as if brushing aside crumbs. "I—I thought I saw Jacob."

"Where?"

"Here. I had washed my husband's work clothes and had them hanging on the line outside."

"As you did today?" Colby asked.

She nodded. "*Yah.* I peered from my window and saw someone grab a shirt and trousers off the clothesline. He glanced up before he ran away, but I do not think he saw me through the glass."

"You told no one?" Becca said.

"I feared Jacob would come back."

"So you recognized the man?" Colby asked. "It was Jacob Yoder?"

Sarah nodded, her eyes wide. "It was Jacob."

"Could it have been Ezekiel instead?" he pressed.

"No."

"How can you be sure?"

Sarah glanced at Becca. "You know Jacob. He is handsome. Remember how you said he made you feel when he looked at you."

Becca's cheeks flushed. She glanced at Colby and then back at Sarah. "Are you sure Jacob stole the clothing?"

"I am sure."

"Did you think he might harm you?" Colby asked.

"*Yah,* I was afraid. I knew about Katie's death. Becca's father, too. Everyone was worried."

"Did you tell the police?"

"I told no one."

"Your husband?" Becca asked.

Sarah shook her head. "I feared for Samuel's safety. He does not know."

"Yet you're telling us this now?"

"Because you were one of us, Rebecca. You will find him."

Becca glanced at Colby. The look of determination on her face told him more than any words could. Jacob Yoder was probably alive, just as she had believed all along. If he had his sights set on Becca, Colby would have to be extra vigilant in order to keep her safe.

SIX

"You're sure it was Jacob Yoder?" Colby asked Frank McDougal, when they were sitting in the living room of his spacious home. The former Harmony sheriff had welcomed Becca and Colby into the three-story stucco with detached garage that made Colby wonder about the pay scale for an Alabama sheriff.

"Yes, I'm sure." McDougal nodded emphatically. "Yoder's body was burned in the house fire, but we were still able to make a visual identification. His wife had become infirmed over the last few years of her life and died in her bed. We ID'd her, as well."

"Was an autopsy performed on either victim?" Becca asked.

McDougal glanced at Colby and shrugged. "We're a small town, far from the big city, but we still do things by the book. However, this time an autopsy wasn't warranted."

Irritated by McDougal's excuses, Colby asked, "Were you aware Jacob Yoder had a brother who was seen in the area just a day prior to the fire?"

The retired cop's gaze narrowed. "It's been eight years. Who told you about a brother?"

"A witness who saw him the day before Jacob died."

A muscle in McDougal's jaw twitched. He leaned in closer. "Where was this witness eight years ago?"

"Did you question the neighbors?" Becca asked.

"I talked to Samuel Hershberger."

"What did he say?"

"That he didn't know who started the fire."

"You suspected arson?" Colby asked.

"We suspected an overturned oil lamp."

Too bad he hadn't talked to Samuel's wife. Colby didn't share the witness's name. If Becca wanted to mention Sarah, she could make that call.

The current sheriff would need to know, but there was something about McDougal's insistence he had identified Jacob that made Colby question if the local law enforcement hadn't cut corners. Claiming Jacob Yoder had died in the house fire solved McDougal's need to close the double-murder case. The former sheriff had been ready to retire. Wrapping up the investigation quickly would have made his last days on the job that much easier.

"Ezekiel Yoder was the same height and build as Jacob," Becca said with determination as if unwilling to cut McDougal any slack. "We'll check with the sheriff's office next to see if there are any records of Ezekiel being seen in the last eight years. I'm sure we won't find anything because you buried him."

She pushed her chair away from the table and stood. "Let me know if you remember anything else, sir."

McDougal frowned. "The case is closed, Rebecca."

"It'll reopen when I arrest Jacob Yoder for killing a man at Fort Rickman, Georgia. The army will want to know who's buried in the Amish cemetery under a tombstone marked with Yoder's name. Be prepared to answer that question because I'll be back." She glanced at Colby. "We'll both be back."

Colby stood, his chest swelling with pride at Becca's assertiveness in dealing with the former sheriff. He followed her to his car.

"Good police work in there," he said as she slid past him into the passenger seat.

"Thanks, but if McDougal had done his job eight years ago, we wouldn't have this problem today. Back then, everything happened too fast. Even I knew that, but I was too grief stricken to ask questions."

She glanced at the sheriff's home. "McDougal was wrong then. He's still wrong."

Colby climbed behind the wheel and inserted the key in the ignition. "You were justified in coming back to Harmony, Becca."

"I needed you in there, Colby. McDougal still considers me a kid from the past. You provided a bigger threat to him."

"Seems you're the one who got his attention." He reached for her hand and wove his fingers through hers to show his support.

"Where to now?" he asked.

"The sheriff's office downtown. It's not far. Head to the main square and then take a left."

Disappointed to learn Lewis Stone, the current sheriff, was out of the office when they arrived, Becca and Colby left their business cards and asked for him to call them once he returned. On the way outside, Colby spotted a sandwich shop at the end of the block.

"Hungry?" he asked.

"Starving."

"Let's grab some chow." They each devoured a burger and fries before hurrying back to Colby's car.

"Elizabeth's house next?" he asked once they buckled their seat belts.

"If you don't mind. I need to pick up my Honda."

Becca stared at the road ahead as Colby drove toward the town square and thought back to the emotional charge he'd felt when they'd both reached for the ketchup at the diner. Just as earlier, he had wrapped his fingers through hers, which caused Becca's cheeks to turn pink and her eyes to widen.

Now he wondered if he had made a mistake.

He needed to stay in control when dealing with Special Agent Miller. They were two professionals, working together. Partners. Yet when he was with her, he felt like their relationship could grow into something more significant.

Once past the square, Colby turned onto the street where Elizabeth lived and parked across from Becca's car.

Opening the passenger door, she smiled back at him. "Elizabeth may want me to come inside for a few minutes."

"I'll wait. I don't want you to be alone if Jacob is on the loose. Besides I'm in no hurry to get to Fort Rickman."

She didn't object, which confirmed that their relationship had improved over the last few hours.

"Give me a few minutes to say goodbye, and then we can be on our way."

Becca knocked on her friend's door, then knocked again with more intensity.

Elizabeth had planned to be home for the rest of the afternoon, but when the door remained closed, Colby stepped to the pavement. Becca glanced back at him for a split second and then turned the knob and peered through the doorway.

"Elizabeth, it's Becca."

Colby hustled toward the house and followed her inside. Silence greeted them.

"Maybe she's in the backyard?" Colby glanced into a large room where a full-size quilt was stretched over a wooden frame. The colors were flamboyant jewel tones accentuated with lush pinks and purples that didn't seem in keeping with someone who had been raised Amish.

Becca pointed through the large bay window to the backyard and drive. "Her car's parked in the rear."

"She could have walked to town, or she might be visiting a neighbor," Colby offered, hoping to calm the anxiety that flashed from Becca's eyes.

"You're probably right." She pulled a notepad and pen from her purse. "I'll leave a note in the kitchen, by the sink. She'll see it there."

Becca stepped into the kitchen.

The paper and pen dropped to the floor. Dread settled over Colby's shoulders. He knew before he entered the room what she'd found.

"I'm so sorry," he murmured as he crossed to where Becca stood, staring down at the older woman—no doubt Elizabeth—sprawled on the tile. The woman's mouth hung open as if she was still screaming at the attacker who had cut her throat and taken her life.

Becca's world spun out of control. She clamped down on her jaw and tried to stem the hot tears that stung her eyes.

"It…it was Jacob," she stammered. Her voice broke. She wrapped her hands around her waist unable to pull her eyes away from her friend's face frozen in fear and disbelief.

Tears flooded her eyes, and she gasped with gut-wrenching sorrow that swept over her like a giant tidal wave.

Colby pulled her close and rubbed his hand over her shoulder, trying to comfort her. With the other, he gripped his cell and called 911. After providing the victim's name and address, he added, "Notify the sheriff that it's a homicide. We need law enforcement on site ASAP."

"Jacob saw my car in front of the house," Becca told Colby once he disconnected. "He probably forced his way in after I left. He was looking for me."

"You can't be sure what happened."

"He followed me from Fort Rickman."

"I was behind you, Becca. I would have noticed him."

She looked at Colby with pain-filled eyes. "Then he followed you."

"I didn't see anyone," he said too quickly. "Besides, Jacob might not be the killer."

She shook her head. "It's him. He's determined to take everyone from me."

Becca wiped her hands over her cheeks and struggled to remain strong. "Elizabeth took me in when I didn't have any place to go. She…she encouraged me to join the military and leave the area. Had I stayed in town, Jacob would have come after me, but she saved me from him then. If only I could have saved her today."

Sirens sounded in the distance. The keening wail cut through the afternoon chill. Becca stared down at Elizabeth's body and the blood that pooled on the kitchen floor. Bending down, she noticed skin under the woman's nails. Her friend had fought back, which meant Jacob would bear visible signs of the attack.

"Thank you for that, Elizabeth." Becca's voice was a whisper. "We'll catch him. I promise."

Colby put his arm around her waist and ushered her toward the foyer. "Let's go outside. We don't want to disturb the crime scene, and we can't do anything for Elizabeth now."

Becca followed him onto the lawn where they flagged down the first patrol car as it rounded the corner. Two additional black-and-whites followed, along with an ambulance.

They showed their identification to the first cop on scene. Colby gave him a quick rundown of what they had found before the officer hustled into the house along with two other cops and the paramedics. One officer remained with Becca and Colby, taking down the information they provided.

Across the street, an old woman peered from the window of her small, one-story, frame home.

"You talk to the cops," Becca told Colby. "I want to question the inquisitive neighbor."

She hurried across the street. A frail woman with gray hair and pale blue eyes opened the door.

Becca flashed her ID and gave her name. "There's nothing to fear, ma'am. We've got lots of law enforcement officers on-site."

"I knew something bad had happened," the woman said.
"How's that?"

"I saw a man that looked suspicious earlier today. My daughter called and I talked to her on the phone for a few minutes. When I hung up and glanced outside again, his car was pulling away from the curb. There was a woman in the passenger seat."

"Could you identify either the driver or the passenger?"

The old woman shook her head. "My eyes aren't the best these days, but there's a car out front that looks identical to the one I saw earlier."

Becca stared at the line-up of vehicles, police and civilian. "Which one?"

"The green sedan."

"Did anyone else stop by Elizabeth's house today?" Becca asked.

"No one else that I saw. Only the people who left in the green car."

Becca's heart sank. The neighbor wasn't going to provide information they needed to apprehend the killer. The car she pointed out had a Fort Rickman decal on the windshield. The older woman had seen a man and woman earlier, but that couple had been Becca and Colby.

Glancing at the police personnel scurrying across Elizabeth's lawn, Becca knew Jacob Yoder had struck again.

She wanted to bring him to justice, but she had no idea where Jacob was or what he was planning to do next.

Lewis Stone, Harmony's current sheriff, arrived on scene some twenty minutes after the first patrol car. He was midforties and wore the same brown uniform as the other men, but four silver stars gleamed from his shirt lapels.

Lewis apologized for being away from his desk earlier when Colby and Becca had stopped by his office. Having grown up in Harmony, he remembered the Mueller murders and listened intently when Becca told him about Ezekiel Yoder and voiced her suspicion that Jacob Yoder was still alive.

"I'll quiz Frank McDougal and see what he can tell me," the sheriff assured her.

Becca relaxed her stance ever so slightly, no doubt relieved to finally have a person in law enforcement who believed her story.

"Sarah Hershberger met Jacob's brother," Colby explained to the sheriff. "You might want to talk to her. From what she said, the two brothers were similar in stature and appearance."

"I'll check with Sarah as well as McDougal. As I recall, that was his last case before retirement."

By nine that night, both Colby and Becca knew they could do nothing more in Harmony. They said goodbye to Lewis and then climbed into their respective cars and headed to Fort Rickman.

The back road to the interstate was a twisty, two-lane that loomed dark and foreboding. Becca had a heavy foot on the gas pedal. Colby followed close behind and flicked his gaze to the narrow shoulder on each side of the paved lanes as well as the stretches of wooded acreage beyond.

They hadn't seen any cars since they'd left Harmony, which underscored the remoteness of the area. Colby was anxious to cross the state line and be back in Georgia.

A road sign warned of an approaching curve. Becca decelerated slightly. Instinctively, he tapped the brake, relieved when his car responded. For a second, he lost sight of her car as she entered a second hairpin turn.

Rounding the curve, Colby saw her vehicle in the middle of the road. He tramped on the brake and screeched to a stop. A tall pine had fallen across the roadway, blocking their progress.

Becca was out of her car before he could caution her to be careful. Stepping onto the pavement, Colby glanced into the dense forest on each side of the road, his internal warning system on high alert.

The sky was clear, the wind calm. No reason for a fallen tree. He unbuttoned the safety on his holster. A sense of foreboding ran up his spine and made him stare even harder into the dark recesses of the night.

"Watch out, Becca," he said as she approached the fallen tree and then turned to face him. "We'll have to move the log off the road."

Inadvertently, she stepped into the arc of illumination from her car's headlights.

Colby's shoulders tensed. "You're exposed, Becca. Get away from the light."

He moved toward her. She stepped aside, but not fast enough.

A shot rang out.

For half a heartbeat, Becca froze.

Colby lunged and shoved her to the pavement. Two more shots pummeled the log. A third pinged against her open driver's door.

A car engine whined in the distance. Tires screeched along a narrow path that paralleled the newer two-lane.

"It was a trap," he said, his tone sharp. "You could have been killed."

She nodded. "I wasn't thinking."

At least, she hadn't been hurt.

"Let's wait a couple minutes before we make any sudden moves just in case someone's hunkered down in the woods."

He listened, but heard only the wind in the pines and the croak of the tree frogs. Satisfied the assailant had left in the car with the squealing tires, Colby scooted off Becca.

"Sorry," he said, hearing her groan.

"Not a problem," she mumbled.

"Keep low while I check out the area." He rose to his knees and stared into the shadowed underbrush.

Her head popped up. "I'm coming with you."

"Becca, please."

"Don't try to baby me, Colby."

"Baby you? I'm trying to keep you alive."

"I can take care of myself."

"Oh, yeah?"

What would have happened if she'd been driving home alone? He visualized Becca's bullet-ridden body bleeding on the pavement just as Elizabeth's lifeblood had darkened her kitchen floor.

Without giving voice to that thought, he hurried back to Becca's car and killed the engine and lights. After grabbing a Maglite from his trunk, he moved forward. Before he could object, Becca was beside him.

Reaching the narrow side road, he shined his light on the pavement and quickly found the black skid marks. Deep tire impressions were visible in the mud where the attacker had more than likely awaited their arrival.

Colby snapped a photo of the tread marks with his phone. "Let's hope forensics can ID the type of tire."

Becca pulled out her phone and snapped her own photos before she called the Harmony sheriff's office and relayed the information to Lewis Stone.

Disconnecting, she glanced at Colby. "Lewis said he'll be here in thirty minutes. Let's put out flares to warn approaching motorists."

Colby flashed his Maglite over the fallen tree trunk. Saw marks were visible. This wasn't a tree that had dropped across the road of its own accord, but a roadblock that had been purposefully set.

A weight settled on Colby's shoulders. Becca hadn't mentioned Jacob's name, but both of them knew he was the most likely suspect.

So far he had failed to harm her, but he would try again.

SEVEN

"Hello, sir." Becca greeted Chief Wilson the next day on the sidewalk leading to the Timmonses' newly built home. A circular drive stretched from the rural road to the two-story brick colonial. Shutters framed the expansive windows that offered views into the main room where a number of guests had already gathered.

After the late night in Alabama, Becca didn't feel like being social, but Dawson and Lillie Timmons had been kind enough to include her and the least she could do was attend the barbecue.

"I appreciate you calling and updating me last night," the chief said as they climbed the stairs to the front porch. "As I mentioned, I'm sorry about your friend who died."

"Thank you, sir. Lewis Stone, the Harmony sheriff, promised to keep us in the loop on both the murder investigation and any information they uncover from the sight of the felled tree."

"You mentioned the Amish man who killed your family members had supposedly been buried some years ago."

"That's right. Jacob Yoder."

"Did Stone think Yoder could still be alive?"

"He didn't offer an opinion one way or the other, but he plans to talk to the former sheriff who identified the body prior to burial."

Wilson pursed his lips. "Special Agent Goodman is looking into a contracting situation that might have bearing on the BOQ explosion. I want him to investigate that lead, while you and Colby follow this one. We'll work both issues until more concrete evidence is revealed." He hesitated.

"You didn't see anyone who looked like this Amish man, did you, Becca?"

"No, sir." She wouldn't mention hearing his voice at the end of the Freemont half marathon. Wilson wanted proof and not a name called out in the midst of a cheering crowd of running enthusiasts.

"Let me know if you hear back from Sheriff Stone."

"Will do, sir."

Dawson Timmons, a beefy blond with twinkling eyes, opened the door before either she or the chief could knock. The two men shook hands. The former special agent invited them inside and smiled when Becca handed him a bouquet of flowers she had purchased at the florist earlier in the morning.

"These are for your wife."

"Lillie loves flowers. Thanks, Becca." He directed them along a hallway. "Follow the chatter. Lillie's in the kitchen. I'm sure she'll want to put the bouquet in water."

Becca trailed Wilson into a large great room where a number of CID personnel were gathered around a small table filled with a sampling of appetizers. A few wives stood to the side and smiled at Becca. The men made room for the chief around the table where the conversation turned to the upcoming Braves baseball season.

From what she could overhear, the women were discussing their children and the local school system. Just like at all parties, the men and women divided into two groups.

Today, Becca couldn't focus on anything except the very real possibility that Jacob Yoder was still alive, which wasn't appropriate conversation for this afternoon gathering. Not feeling part of either group, she grabbed a chip off a nearby table to cover the awkwardness of standing alone in a roomful of people.

"Try the artichoke dip." Colby appeared at her side.

"It looks good." She smiled.

Colby had a knack for showing up when she felt most vulnerable. In the past, she hadn't appreciated his timeliness. That wasn't the case today.

Following his lead, she scooped a large dollop of dip onto a chip and took a bite, appreciating the rich mix of flavors.

"How are you?" His gaze was filled with concern.

"A little tired, but fine otherwise."

"Long night."

"For both of us." She thought of Elizabeth and her throat tightened.

As if sensing her upset, Colby pointed through the sliding glass doors to the expansive deck that stretched along the back of the house. "Drinks are in the cooler outside. May I get you something?"

"Bottled water, if they have it. Otherwise a soda."

He squeezed her arm before he headed to the deck. Returning, he carried two waters, which he opened then handed one to her.

"Are you always so thoughtful?" she asked.

"My sisters claim they trained me well." His smiled revealed their close relationship. "In reality, I'm just a sensitive guy." He winked, sending a ripple of warmth to circle her heart.

"An officer and a gentleman, right?" Becca repeated the army phrase.

His smile grew even wider. "Always."

Her cheeks burned, and she took a long drink of the chilled water. Cognitively she knew Colby was laying on the charm, but she enjoyed the slight shift in their relationship, especially since they were away from the office and at a social event. Fatigue probably helped to weaken her defenses. Or perhaps after what they had experienced together yesterday, she was feeling more at ease with Colby at her side.

Even without his sisters' stamp of approval, she knew he was a good guy who she could trust. Although with his rugged good looks and outgoing personality, he probably had a string of women trying to catch his eye.

Somewhat unsettled by the thought, she reached for another chip, needing to hide the confusion attacking her midsection. Maybe Colby was already spoken for at this point in his life. Some petite blonde who didn't carry a gun or look over her shoulder whenever she got out of a car.

"You know everyone, don't you?" He glanced around the room, seemingly oblivious to her internal struggle.

She followed his gaze, hoping to refocus her attention on the invited guests. She knew the CID personnel and had met most of the wives at the post-wide Hail and Farewell when she had first arrived at the fort.

An older woman appeared from the kitchen and placed a tray of stuffed mushrooms on the table.

Colby leaned closer, which sent Becca into a momentary tailspin as she inhaled a lemon-lime scent that was totally masculine.

"That's Lillie's mom." He lowered his voice so only she could hear. "Her dad's helping in the kitchen. I'll introduce you."

Knowing close proximity to Colby could be dangerous, at least to her mental well-being, Becca kept space between them as they walked through the dining room and into the kitchen beyond, relieved to be doing something other than breathing in his yummy aftershave.

They found Lillie standing behind a granite-topped island in the kitchen, wearing a wide smile and a flowered dress. She wiped her hands on a cloth and then scurried forward to give Becca a hug. "The flowers are lovely. You shouldn't have."

"It's the least I could do."

"I want you to meet my parents." Lillie introduced the Beaumonts, who were just as Colby had said, caring folks whose words of welcome put Becca at ease.

Seeing how they hovered around their daughter caused a tug at Becca's heart for what had never been part of her own life. As much as Becca needed to forgive the past, she couldn't let go of the bad decisions her father had made concerning his children as well as the pain of his rejection. If only he had believed her when she had told him about Jacob's desire to have his way with her. Becca had fought off Jacob's advances, without the help of her *datt,* who had ignored the danger and provided her with no other recourse than to flee. Regrettably, Katie had been left behind to suffer the consequences of Jacob's anger that led to her death two years later. Now Elizabeth was another casualty.

"The grill's hot." Entering the kitchen, Dawson flashed an endearing smile at his pretty wife whose expression reflected the love between them, causing another tug at Becca's heart.

He lifted the roasting pan filled with ribs off the counter, then pointed to a second pan and nodded to Colby. "Lillie cooked the ribs in the oven, but they still need barbecue sauce and a good searing on the grill. Mind giving me a hand?"

"Not a problem." Grabbing the second pan of ribs, Colby followed Dawson through the back door that led to the deck.

"Do you need help?" Becca asked Lillie once the men had left the room.

Mrs. Beaumont smiled warmly and placed a large bowl of potato salad into Becca's outstretched hands. "This needs to go on the dining room table."

Becca did as Mrs. Beaumont asked and returned to the kitchen, thankful to be of service.

"How was the race yesterday?" Lillie pulled a bowl of colorful congealed gelatin salad from the refrigerator.

"You were there?" Becca asked over her shoulder as she headed back to the table with the gelatin.

Lillie shook her head. "Dawson and I were getting things ready here, but we saw your photo in the local paper."

Becca tucked a stray stand of hair behind her ear. "I—I wasn't aware anyone took my picture."

"The photo was taken last week when you were signing up to run." Lillie shuffled through the papers on a nearby desk. "Here it is."

The photo showed Becca at the Freemont City Hall, filling out the race forms.

"You might be able to get additional copies from the newspaper office downtown if you want to mail them to family," Lillie suggested.

"One copy is all I need." Becca didn't have any other family members, but she was concerned that someone had seen the photo. Someone from her past. Someone she had been hiding from for eight years.

Colby entered the kitchen, carrying the now-empty roasting pans. "Dawson needs a plate for the ribs."

Lillie handed him a serving platter. "Remind him I like them good and done."

"I'll pass that on." Colby laughed. "But I might need Becca to back me up."

"Go ahead." Lillie motioned both of them outside. "The table's ready. We're just waiting for the meat."

The weather was almost like spring when they stepped outside, though dark clouds hovered in the distance. Becca inhaled deeply, lifting her face to the warmth, glad to have a few minutes to enjoy the sunshine.

The rolling pastures brought back memories of the fields on her father's farm, although his acreage had never been productive, and he had bemoaned the ground on more than one occasion. He had also lamented that his girls had not been the sons he wanted and needed to manage the farm.

A number of people stood near the grill and watched Dawson flip the ribs, basting both sides. The fire sizzled, and the scent of tangy barbecue sauce and roasted meat filled the air.

Becca turned her attention to the winding country road in the distance. Her gaze narrowed as she spied something unusual for this part of Georgia. The muscles in her neck tightened, and her heart skittered in her chest. On the rise of a far hill, a horse-drawn buggy clip-clopped along the horizon.

"What you looking at?" Colby came up behind her.

Caught off guard by his nearness, she shook her head. "Nothing in particular. Just enjoying the idyllic setting."

He inhaled deeply. "The sunshine feels good, although we might have rain before long." He pointed to the dark clouds.

A flurry of activity at the grill caused him to turn. He touched her arm. "Dawson's taking the ribs inside."

"I'll be right there."

She glanced again at the horse-drawn buggy and shivered, not from the cool breeze that had picked up in the last few minutes, but from what the buggy signified. If the Amish had moved into this area of Georgia, someone could be part of that new community. A man she had never wanted to see again. Jacob Yoder.

If he had seen her photo in the paper, he could have make inquiries about the location of where she lived. Surprised by Ralph Arnold once he had broken in the unoccupied apartment, Jacob could have rigged the explosion that had claimed the project manager's life.

Becca had been so careful for so long, but coming back to the South could have placed her in Jacob's path. Two people had died and attempts had been made on her own life. She needed to find Jacob, and the buggy might provide a clue to his whereabouts.

"I want to thank all of you for being with us today," Dawson said when Becca joined the guests inside. "I also want to ask God's blessing on the food."

Colby stared at Becca from the other side of the circle. Not wanting to reveal the mix of emotions welling up within her, she lowered her head and folded her hands while Dawson gave thanks for the food they were about to eat, for the military and CID and for all those in uniform who served. At the conclusion of his prayer, everyone joined in a heartfelt "Amen."

Dawson pointed them toward the dining room. "Ladies and gentlemen, please grab a plate and get some chow."

The people filed through the line and headed for the more casual but comfortable family room where they sat around two long folding tables.

Lillie handed out additional napkins to wipe the barbecue sauce from their sticky fingers. "Delicious," many said as they enjoyed the meaty ribs.

Chief Wilson sat back once he had finished eating and chuckled when Dawson took his empty plate. "I never knew you had culinary skills when you were with the CID"

"It's Lillie, sir. She taught me everything I know." He glanced at his wife across the room and winked. She responded with a fetching smile that wasn't lost on Becca.

From the hint of longing that flashed momentarily across Colby's face, he too had noticed the intimate exchange.

"Thanks for inviting us here today," the chief said. "It's nice to be in the country."

He pointed toward the deck. "I'm not sure how many of you saw the horse and buggy on that distant farm road when Dawson was taking the ribs off the grill."

"I heard there's a new Amish community in the area," one of the men mentioned.

Wilson nodded in agreement. "As you know, the commanding general is committed to working with the Freemont community. To further that goal, he's interested in hosting a farmers' market and craft fair. His wife is spearheading a taskforce of folks to organize the first event to be held in the field beside the Fort Rickman museum. Mrs. Cameron asked us to work with the military police to provide security. I'll need someone from the CID to represent us on the committee. If anyone's interested, let me know."

"Sir, do you have any idea how many families are in the community and where they came from?" Becca asked.

"I should have more information in the next day or so. I'll let you know what I find out."

"Thank you, sir."

Lillie excused herself to prepare the dessert. Becca followed her to the kitchen with her empty plate in hand.

"Did you save room for red velvet cake?" Lillie opened the freezer and pulled out a container of ice cream. A large cake with cream-cheese icing sat on the counter.

"I'm too full from the wonderful meal. Thank you for a delightful afternoon."

"Do you have to get back to post?" Dawson asked as he entered the kitchen.

"I'm afraid so. Everything was lovely. I appreciate you including me."

Becca left through the kitchen door and hurried to her car. Instead of returning to Fort Rickman, she planned to head in the direction the buggy had gone earlier, hoping the road would lead to the Amish community.

If Jacob Yoder were still alive, would it be too much of a coincidence to have him living close to Freemont and neighboring Fort Rickman?

Becca had spent eight years hiding out in foreign countries to elude his wrath, but she wouldn't live her life looking over her shoulder any longer. From now on, she would take back the life he had ruined.

Glancing at the Timmonses' home, she thought of Colby and his desire to help her. He'd supported her when she found Elizabeth's body and had shoved her out of the line of fire later that night. They were supposed to be working together, but leaving without him seemed the best option. She didn't want him to get involved.

Then she thought of his strong arms and steady gaze and the way her heart fluttered when she smelled his aftershave. Was she making a mistake by excluding him today?

When Becca didn't return to the family room, Colby excused himself and headed for the kitchen where he found Lillie arranging ice cream and cake on desert dishes. Her mother stood at a nearby counter and poured cream into a small pitcher, which she placed next to a sugar bowl on a large serving tray.

"Dessert's almost ready," Lillie said as she rinsed his dinner plate in the sink.

"I'll have to pass, although it looks delicious." He glanced around the kitchen. "I thought Becca Miller was with you."

"She left a few minutes ago."

Colby thanked Lillie and then stretched out his hand to Dawson before he hastened from the house. Had mention of the Amish community upset Becca?

Focused on picking up her trail, he opened his car door and sighed with relief when he saw her sitting in the passenger seat.

She smiled coyly. "I knew you'd follow me so I decided if we're a team, we'd better stick together."

Slipping behind the wheel, he clicked on his seat belt. "Good decision. We'll come back for your car later. Right now, I presume you want to go to the new Amish community."

"Seems we're thinking alike."

As he pulled out of the driveway, Colby knew they'd overcome a huge hurdle. Becca had realized they could work together. If Jacob Yoder was still alive, she'd need backup and another set of eyes to keep her safe. Hopefully, she'd want him around for other reasons, as well. Becca had gotten to him, but in a good way, and Colby wanted to be the person she needed most of all.

EIGHT

The road Becca and Colby followed eventually spilled into an area dotted with farms on both sides. As Colby drove, she stared out the window, thinking back to house raisings in Harmony, when neighbors gathered to help new families get started.

Hard work was an Amish trait, which her father hadn't inherited. Instead, he bemoaned the lack of sons, causing Becca to overcompensate and try to do the manual labor as well as maintain the house. No matter how hard she tried, she could never do enough to please him. When he had ordered her to accept Jacob Yoder's offer to keep house for his sickly wife, Becca had hoped things would change. Regrettably, they had only gotten worse.

In the distance, she spied a number of buggies parked beside a farmhouse and a newly built barn.

"What's going on?" Colby asked.

"Looks like a barn raising. Everyone comes together to help."

"That's a great way to share the load."

"As a child, I loved gathering for such an event," Becca reminisced. "After the work was done, the children were allowed to romp outdoors while the adults visited."

Colby's eyes twinkled as he glanced at her. "I know you were cute in your long skirt and apron."

"I was too tall and much too thin. *Gangly* would be the best word to describe me. My mother said I'd eventually grow into my body, although she didn't live long enough to see me through that awkward stage."

"You probably tried to fill your mother's shoes."

"And didn't succeed. My father said I was the cross he had to bear."

"That's tough on a kid." Colby shrugged. "On anyone."

"He was never a happy man, but his temperament changed after my mother died. He'd injured his back some years earlier and was besieged with pain. Plus, the farm work was more than we could handle. Katie and I helped, but in his opinion, we never did enough."

They passed the farmhouse with the buggies in the front yard and continued on, studying the homes that dotted the sides of the road. The farms were not large by *English* standards, but each provided ample acreage for the crops and livestock needed to feed a family and cover the cost of necessities as well as the mortgage and taxes for the land.

"I don't want to give you the wrong opinion, Colby. The Amish way is not easy, but it has its own rewards."

"I can see that. In fact, while Dawson was grilling, he talked about the satisfaction of working the land and providing for his family. There's something to say about the simple lifestyle. In fact, the Amish way reminds me of the military with its adherence to rules and high moral code. Too few people hold on to virtue these days. That's something to say for both the military and the Amish."

Regrettably, Jacob Yoder and her father were exceptions to the rule.

Running out of farmland as they approached an intersection, Becca said, "Turn left onto that dirt road. It looks like there's a farm tucked behind that thicket of trees."

Just as she suspected, the thick crop of hardwoods eventually opened into a clearing. A farmhouse, not as large or as well cared for as some of the others, sat in the open space, surrounded by pastures and a small creek. A few head of cattle grazed in a nearby meadow oblivious to the newcomers who pulled into the drive to turn around.

The absence of power and telephone lines confirmed

Becca's hunch of this being an Amish home. The house's need for paint brought back other memories from her past.

A barn sat at the side of the property. The door hung on one hinge and flapped in the wind. Dogs barked in the distance.

Becca shivered as she studied the landscape.

"Cold?" Colby asked.

"I'm fine."

He stared at her for a long moment. "You look pale. Is something wrong?"

She shook her head and wrapped her arms around her waist. Another gust of wind forced the barn door to fly back with a bang.

Colby glanced at the darkening sky. "Those clouds look threatening. The farmer's probably at the barn raising. I'd better secure the barn door before the downpour hits."

"I'll go with you."

Becca stepped from the car and inhaled the damp air that signaled the approaching rain. She studied the landscape. Nothing moved, other than the wind through the trees. Even the dogs were silent.

Placing her purse strap around her neck, she felt the weight of her weapon holstered inside. No matter how peaceful the setting, Jacob Yoder could be nearby.

Flicking her gaze over the house and surrounding area, she walked with Colby toward the barn, taking care to silence her footfalls in the winter grass.

As she neared the corner of the house, the dogs started to bark again. She turned to see the chain-link pen that kept them bound, and let out a deep sigh of relief. The dogs— both Doberman pinschers—had jaws large enough to take off her hand. She shivered, then hurried to join Colby.

Glancing into the barn's dim interior, she saw something that shouldn't have been on an Amish farm.

A late-model Crown Victoria, metallic blue in color.

She stooped to examine the tires, thick with red clay. The car had been stuck in the mud recently.

Pulling her phone from her purse, she snapped photos of the tires and the tread marks on the barn's dirt floor. She also photographed the front grill and trunk that lacked plates.

Pointing to the house, she said, "Let's see if anyone's home. I want to find out more about the car." Specifically, she wanted to know who owned the Crown Vic and whether it had been driven to Alabama the day before. The lack of plates brought other questions to mind.

Colby closed and latched the barn and followed Becca to the house. She knocked repeatedly. When no one answered, they returned to the car and drove back the way they came.

Approaching the farmhouse with the newly built barn, Colby pulled to the side of the road.

As if oblivious to the darkening sky, children frolicked on the lawn while the adults chatted nearby. Just as at Dawson's house, the men and women stood in separate groups. A few folks glanced their way and then returned to their conversations.

A man helped a woman into their buggy. After taking his seat, he slapped the reins and the horses stared down the drive. Becca and Colby stepped from the car and held up their identification.

The man hesitated as if weighing whether to stop.

Becca raised her voice. "I'm with the Criminal Investigation Division at Fort Rickman." She pointed to Colby and introduced him before she continued. "You folks know a man named Jacob Yoder? He's six-two, black hair, brown eyes with a small scar on his left cheek."

The Amish man shook his head.

"He's in his mid-thirties," she pressed. "Formerly, he lived in Harmony, Alabama."

"I cannot help you."

She thought of Elizabeth. "He could have scratches to his face and hands."

"I have not seen such a man."

"Do you know who lives in the last farm on the left? Two Dobermans are caged behind the house? A blue Crown Vic is parked in the barn?"

The bearded man shook his head again. "This does not sound like an Amish family." Raising the reins, he clucked his tongue to signal the horses. The buggy creaked forward.

Becca watched it jostle along the road, regretting the Amish need to remain separate from the world and less than forthright with the *English*. Privacy was part of the Amish way, a way that would hinder their investigation.

She turned her gaze back to the hillside. An older woman, her gray hair caught up in a *kapp* bonnet, left the house. She stopped and stared at Becca for a long moment before she joined the other women.

Fat drops of rain began to fall. The people scurried for shelter. Some folks ran for the barn while others grabbed their children and hoisted them into their rigs before climbing in themselves.

Becca and Colby returned to his car and wiped the rain from their faces before he pulled back onto the road. Becca glanced over her shoulder and watched the buggies head in the opposite direction. If only someone had information about a man from her past who wanted to do her harm.

Was Jacob hiding out among the Amish?

NINE

Becca was besieged with dreams of Amish buggies and shots being fired at her in the darkness. A strange, wizened woman, wearing a white *kapp,* sat behind the wheel of a Ford Crown Victoria and accelerated straight toward her.

She woke Monday morning in a cold sweat and glanced at her weapon on the nightstand.

Pulling herself upright, Becca dangled her feet over the side of the mattress and listened expectantly.

A *rap-tap-tap* sounded in the stillness.

She grabbed her Glock and tiptoed to the door.

"Becca, it's Colby." His voice was a whisper, but easy enough to recognize.

"What do you want?"

"To talk."

"Now?" She glanced at the bedside clock. Five in the morning was too early to play nice.

"Yes, now."

She moved aside the straight-back chair she'd shimmied under the door knob as an extra barrier and turned the dead bolt. Inching the door open, she kept the chain guard in place and peered with one eye through the small slit. "What's going on?"

He held up his hands. "Trust me, Becca. I've got a good reason for being here."

"Then start talking."

"I searched the archived newspaper reports of your father's and sister's deaths and found information about Jacob Yoder. He grew up in Pinecraft, Florida, an area in Sarasota. His brother did, as well."

"What's that got to do with me?"

"I'm driving there today. Wilson gave me the go-ahead. I told him you'd probably want to go, as well."

"How long will it take?"

"Five hours to get there. We'll spend the night and head back tomorrow."

She stared at Colby for a long moment, weighing her options. Stay on post or find out information about the Yoder brothers?

"Give me ten minutes. I'll meet you in the lobby."

She closed the door and stood for a moment, waiting to hear Colby's footfalls as he headed downstairs.

Spending two days with the special agent might put her in an awkward position. She and Colby both needed to understand the rules. They were investigating two murders that could tie in with four additional deaths.

Becca was interested. Who in law enforcement wouldn't be? But spending all that time with Colby could be a problem, if he didn't see her as a special agent doing her job and nothing more.

Then she realized the problem wasn't with Colby. It was with her.

Colby checked his watch when he heard footsteps coming down the stairs in the Lodge. Becca appeared wearing a flowing skirt and matching sweater set and lightweight jacket. She'd pulled her hair back from her face and carried a small overnight bag along with her purse.

"You dressed and packed in nine minutes? I'm impressed." He smiled.

"I've done it in less time."

The woman never cut herself any slack.

He reached for her overnight bag and was surprised when she let him carry it for her. Another step in the right direction.

"My car's out front." He motioned her toward the door, which he opened.

The chilly morning greeted them. Becca slipped into the passenger seat while he placed her bag in the trunk. Rounding the car, he climbed behind the wheel, noting the flowery scent that hung in the air. The Amish-girl-turned-cop wore nice perfume. That tiny glimpse into the real Becca behind the reticent facade made him smile.

He handed her a map. "We'll pick up Interstate 75 and drive south to Sarasota. At that point, I may need help with directions."

"What about GPS?"

He patted his console. "Tucked away in case I ever need it. Call me old-fashioned, but I still prefer maps."

"Thank you, Uncle Sam."

"Pardon?" He raised his brow unsure of what she meant.

"We work with maps in the army. No wonder you're more comfortable using them."

"Right." He pulled out of the parking lot and increased his speed when they left post. Once they were on the interstate, he mentioned Pinecraft.

"Did you hear about the area growing up?" he asked.

She laughed ruefully. "Never. We were just trying to survive. Vacations weren't even considered." She paused for a moment and looked out the window. "I often wondered what the ocean looked like. A farm girl from Alabama, especially coming for such a limited environment…"

She shrugged. "I never thought I'd get beyond Harmony. The army expanded my horizons. I did a lot of traveling when I was stationed in Europe. My first trip was to the Mediterranean for a week-long tour run by Morale Support."

"You traveled alone?"

"With someone else in law enforcement."

Colby shifted in his seat, wondering about her European

traveling companion. "Some guy you dated?" The question slipped out unexpectedly.

"A woman who worked with the military police. She was a quiet type, and we got along."

Although relieved that she hadn't traveled with a boyfriend, Colby could imagine the number of guys who tried to catch Becca's eye. Who wouldn't? She was pretty in an unassuming way.

"The ocean was always my favorite destination," she continued, seemingly oblivious to his musings about her possible boyfriends. "I loved seeing everything. Rome, Venice, the Black Forest in Germany. Each was unique and special in its own way."

"Nice you took the opportunity to travel."

"You didn't?"

"I've been in Afghanistan on four deployments. Never got to Europe."

"But you've traveled in the U.S."

He nodded. "And spent lots of time at the beach. My sisters love the water."

She smiled. "No one's married yet?"

"My sisters are too independent."

"Sounds as if you don't approve."

"Hardly. The problem comes when they try to tell *me* what to do."

Becca's laughter filled the car with a lightness he hadn't felt in a long time.

"I'm the second from the eldest. My older sister is the only one who pushes the issue." He smiled, thinking of Gloria. "She wants me to settle down."

"Yet she's still single."

"There was a guy. She was head over heels in love with him. We all thought the feeling was mutual. They planned the wedding. The invitations were sent. The gifts had started to arrive. He texted her two days before the ceremony saying he'd found someone else."

Becca turned to look at Colby. "He sounds like a louse."

"I thought as much, but what could I tell her?"

"Now she's protecting her heart," Becca said.

"Exactly. There's a nice guy who keeps hanging around, but I don't think he'll wait much longer."

"You've talked to her?"

"As much as I can. After a point, she closed the door. Better to pull back a bit on the brotherly advice so the door remains open. I've learned to pick my battles."

"She's lucky to have you." There was sincerity in Becca's voice.

"The feeling's mutual, but I worry about her. I don't want her to throw away something good because of fear."

Becca nodded. "Fear can hold anyone back."

He glanced at her, thinking of the fear he'd seen in her eyes the night of the fire. She'd mentioned Jacob. At least now, he knew she had suspected Jacob Yoder right from the start.

Glancing down, Becca picked at the sleeve of her jacket. "My sister and I were close. Katie was two years younger and everything I wasn't. She had a gentle spirit that made her seem vulnerable. That worried me. I wanted her to be a little tougher and stand up for herself."

"You can't blame yourself."

"I blame myself for leaving. It was easier to escape than to change the way things were."

She tugged at her hair. "My father forced Katie to take my place working at the Yoder home after I left. Jacob paid well. Too well. My father didn't understand his dark motives."

Glancing out the window, she sighed. "Maybe he didn't want to see. I had trouble getting away from Jacob. My sister wasn't as strong as I was, so I can only imagine what happened."

"Not all men are self-serving, Becca."

"I know that."

Did she? Or was she too hung up on the past?

She eased her head back on the seat and stared out the window as if to close the door on their conversation. Colby tapped on the cruise control. Traffic was steady with a long string of trucks heading south. He needed to focus on the road and not the attractive woman sitting next to him.

They would have time later to talk about her past and Jacob Yoder and whether Becca was still hanging on to the hurt. Right now, he'd give her space to be in her own world. Hopefully, once they arrived in Pinecraft, they'd find information about Jacob and his brother. If Ezekiel was still alive, they'd be back at the beginning of the investigation with no leads to follow.

Jacob Yoder was a long shot, but his was the only name they had to go on.

Besides, Becca seemed sure he was still alive. And after everything that had happened, Colby had to agree.

TEN

Colby didn't mind the drive, and the hours flew by along with the miles. Becca remained quiet for most of the trip, but the silence was comfortable as if borne from familiarity. At one point, her head drooped against her shoulder, and he realized she was asleep.

The frown lines he saw too often were replaced with a peaceful beauty he found endearing. Becca didn't flaunt flashy good looks, but she had a sweet aura that called to him.

Of course, he had also seen the anxiety and concern written too clearly on her face when she talked about a killer on the loose. Maybe Colby was drawn to the vulnerability she would never admit to having.

His sisters claimed he was overprotective. They laughed when he became too concerned about their well-being or questioned them too extensively about who they were dating and where they were going. He'd learned from his father, and now that Colby was older, he shared the male guardian role along with his dad.

Thinking back to Afghanistan and Ellen, he shook his head ever so slightly. Her self-sufficiency had butted heads with his need to keep her safe. She'd been adamant about not wanting his help. In hindsight, he realized his pride had gotten in the way and caused him to walk away from her when she'd needed him most.

He sighed as if trying to release the painful memory.

"Is there a problem?" Becca asked, her voice thick with sleep.

He turned and smiled at the look of concern she wore so openly. "I woke you. Sorry."

"I must have drifted off."

She glanced at the surrounding traffic, and the city that sprawled out in every direction from the freeway. "If this is Sarasota, I did more than doze."

"You fell asleep after we got gas in Wildwood."

"I should have been checking the map."

"It's been an easy drive," he assured her. "Our exit is just ahead."

The winter sun shone through the windows and warmed the car. Becca slipped out of her coat.

"Ready for air-conditioning?" Colby asked with a smile.

"Actually, I'm fine, although fresh air might be nice." She cracked the window on her side and inhaled deeply. "Do I smell salt water or am I imagining we're not far from the Gulf?"

"About six or seven miles," Colby said. "We can head there later today, after we check out Pinecraft. I thought we'd stop at one of the diners and ask a few questions first. From what I've read, the area is a melting pot for Amish and Mennonite folks from around the country. They seem to let down some barriers when they're on vacation."

"Meaning they'll share information."

"That's what I'm hoping."

Colby exited the freeway and ended up on the east-west thoroughfare. Passing Oak View Drive on the left, they took the next major right into a community of small bungalows and a scattering of shops. Mobile homes were nestled in between modest cinder-block homes where palm trees and flowering shrubs added color and texture to the eclectic neighborhood.

Three-wheeled bicycles were parked in front of a restaurant that served Pennsylvania Dutch cooking. A sign in the window read, *"Schmeckt mir gut."*

"Loosely translated it means the food tastes good," Becca told him.

"Looks like the crowd agrees." Colby pointed to the clusters of people milling around in the parking lot.

A number of the men were dressed in denim overalls and straw hats. Others wore white shirts and dark trousers held up with suspenders. The majority of men had beards that partially covered their weatherworn faces.

The women wore simple dresses and sturdy shoes. Some had white bonnets and aprons. Others piled their hair in large buns at the back of their neck. The loose strands blew around their faces in the gentle breeze.

"Let's get lunch and see if anyone remembers the Yoder family." Colby pulled into a vacant parking space and stepped from the car.

After the long drive, Colby wondered if coming to Pinecraft had been a good idea. He glanced at Becca. Once again, her face was marked with worry. If only the trip would provide information they needed about Jacob Yoder and his brother. Maybe then she could forget the past and move on with her future.

Becca opened the car door and hesitated a moment, eying an unleashed dog nearby. Waiting until the mutt passed by, she turned to find Colby watching her.

Shifting away from his gaze, she studied the gathering of plain folks, whose friendly chatter and laughter seemed infectious. For a fleeting moment, Becca longed to recapture the essence of her youth. The simple dresses and open faces, all fresh and natural, tugged at the memories she held in the deep recesses of her heart.

A young woman, standing with a number of teens, reminded her of Katie, with her trim body and warm smile.

Becca waved to the small child in an older woman's arms. The toddler giggled and then hid his face against his mother's neck.

Colby touched her arm. He leaned toward her, close

enough that she could smell his aftershave. "Too many memories?"

She shook her head. "I'm fine." But she wasn't. She was struck again with the pain of loss. Katie had been such a sweet soul. She should have married well and had a houseful of children of her own. Instead, she had been murdered. All the possibilities of what could have been had ended that terrible night Jacob Yoder forced his way into their home.

If only Becca could have arrived earlier. She could have saved Katie or sent her scurrying into the night away from danger.

Instead Jacob had found her sister, hiding in the pantry.

"Becca." Colby's voice was laced with concern.

She pulled in a ragged breath and focused on the wooden walkway leading to the restaurant. "We'd better get a table before everyone realizes it's lunchtime."

A young woman in a light blue dress and apron showed them to a booth by the window. For a long moment, they watched the flow of traffic on the main road and the influx of people who biked or walked toward the restaurant.

"I would never expect so many Amish to gather here," Becca said. "In Harmony, the Amish kept to themselves. Here it seems they mix with everyone."

"The information I read said many of the folks bus to Pinecraft each year. They rent homes in the area and make friends with people from all over the country."

"They seem so opposite from the closed communities farther north." She thought of her own hesitancy to reveal the truth about Jacob Yoder years ago until he'd become such a threat that she had to tell her father.

What would have happened, if she'd been forthright and gotten help from the local authorities? Would McDougal have listened to an Amish girl who claimed a married man had tried to touch her?

Naive as she had been back then, she would have choked

on the words and would never have been able to describe
how he had lured her to the barn and forced her down onto
the hay and tried to have his way with her.

So many people didn't understand why she had run away
from Harmony. She wasn't running away from the Amish
way of life per se. She was running away from Jacob.

He had warned her when she first went to work for him
that she could never run away. He would find her. Which is
exactly what he had done.

"A penny for your thoughts," Colby said from across
the table.

Becca shook her head. "Sorry, I was thinking back to
Harmony."

"You'll feel better after you eat."

They both studied the expansive menu.

"I'll have the chicken with homemade noodles, mashed
potatoes and gravy," Becca told the waitress when she returned to take their order.

"Meat loaf with the same sides." He looked at Becca.
"Iced tea?"

"Please."

The waitress, a middle-aged woman with rosy cheeks,
brought two glasses of tea and a basket of freshly baked rolls
still warm from the oven.

"I may go into carb overload," Becca said as she placed
a plump roll on her bread plate.

Colby did the same, and before he reached for the butter,
he noted a family sitting at the next table. The four young
children sat still as the parents bowed their heads and offered
a blessing over the food they were about to eat.

"My father leads the grace at our house," Colby shared.
The memory brought a warm spot to his heart. He'd forsaken
prayer since his first deployment. Somehow thanking God

hadn't seemed necessary in a war zone, which in retrospect was the most obvious place to include God.

Colby had survived four tours and too many close calls to count. He joked that his mom and dad and sisters' prayers had brought him home safe and sound from each deployment, yet he himself had given the Lord only the scantest attention in all that time. Dawson's prayer yesterday had seem fitting, and here, in this family-style restaurant, the need to invoke the Lord seemed fitting, as well.

"I don't suppose you'd want to offer a blessing?" he asked Becca.

She shook her head. "Go ahead. You lead."

So much for trying to pass the buck. He cleared his throat and lowered his gaze. "Father God, thank You for our safe journey this morning and for the warm welcome at this restaurant. We ask Your blessing on the food we are about to eat and on those who prepared it. Lead us to information about the Yoder brothers and keep us safe as we do our job." He glanced up, seeing her bowed head and closed eyes.

"Amen," they murmured in unison.

As if she had been waiting for the conclusion of their blessing, the waitress appeared almost immediately with their plates.

Colby's mouth watered at the savory aroma and the huge servings. "Do you cook like this?" he asked Becca.

She shook her head and stared at her plate. "I should have asked for a child's portion."

The food was as delicious as it was bountiful, and they both ate with relish.

"My mother makes a mean meat loaf, but nothing this good," Colby said as he reached for his tea.

"Which you shouldn't mention when you call home."

He laughed. "I know when to be tactful."

She paused, a forkful of mashed potatoes halfway to her mouth. "You're very considerate, Colby."

Considerate? He'd take that as a compliment, although he hoped she saw other attributes in him as well, which he continued to mull over as he finished eating.

At the conclusion of the meal, he sighed with contentment. "My father says a man works better with a full stomach."

Becca laughed. "I'm not sure that applies to women."

She opened her purse, but Colby held up his hand. "I've got the check."

He motioned to the waitress who hurried to the table.

"You enjoyed the food?" she asked, reaching for his plate.

"We did. Thank you." He eyed her name tag. "Miriam, we're trying to locate the Yoder family. They had two sons Ezekiel and Jacob. Both would be in their mid-thirties by now."

"They live in Pinecraft?"

"Years ago they did. Jacob went north to Alabama at some point. I'm not sure what happened to Ezekiel."

The waitress nodded. "I'll check with the other staff, but I do not know the family of which you speak, although Yoder is a common name. There's a Yoder's restaurant in the area, but they do not have sons those ages."

When the waitress left the table, Becca said to Colby, "We need to find an older person who might remember the Yoders we're looking for."

He gazed through the window at a nearby vegetable market and convenience store. "Let's keep asking until we find someone who does remember."

The waitress returned shaking her head. "Everyone who works here has only come to the area in the last ten years or so. There was an older family named Yoder that moved north some time ago."

"Did they have sons?"

"Three girls."

Colby paid the check, and both he and Becca thanked the

waitress for her help. After leaving the restaurant, they hurried across the parking lot to the marketplace.

An Amish man in his thirties greeted them with a warm smile. "May I help you?"

After explaining their need for information, he shook his head. "I knew a Yoder family in Ohio, but no one by that name in the local area." He pointed to one of the side streets. "Hershel Trotter and his wife have lived in Pinecraft for many years and rent rooms on the next street over. They might be of help."

Leaving their car, Colby and Becca walked to the house the clerk in the market had described. A small sign in the front yard read Rooms for Rent.

The sound of voices drew them to the backyard. Four couples—the men in denim overalls and women in simple dresses—stood around two shuffleboard courts. A hefty man, mid-fifties with gray hair and an equally gray beard, shoved his puck down the court. His lie was good, and he received shouts of encouragement from the others.

One of the men turned as Becca and Colby approached.

"Good day." Becca nodded to the man and his wife. She glanced at the other couples who had halted their revelry and were peering with questioning eyes at the special agents.

Colby let Becca take the lead, knowing her Amish roots would put her in better stead.

After introducing herself and Colby, she held up her CID identification. "We're searching for information about a family that lived in Pinecraft fifteen to twenty years ago by the name of Yoder."

The man eyed them with skepticism and shook his head. "Yoder is a common name."

"Jacob and Ezekiel were the sons," Becca offered.

"Perhaps Herschel knows them."

As if having heard his name mentioned, a man—no

doubt, Herschel—stuck his head out the back door. *"Wie-gates?"*

One of the men pointed to Becca and Colby. "These people are looking for someone named Yoder who lived here years ago."

"Abram Yoder?" Herschel asked as he stepped onto the back stoop.

"We only know the names of the Yoder sons," Becca said. "Jacob and Ezekiel."

"Yah, that would be Abram Yoder's family."

"Where is Abram now?" Colby asked.

"With the Lord. He moved north and died some years ago."

"Do you have information about his family?"

"Abram was a quiet man who kept to himself."

If only Mr. Trotter would be more forthcoming.

Colby stepped closer. "Sir, do you know anyone who might have information about the sons?"

Trotter rubbed his beard and stared into the sky. "Sally Schrock would know."

"Where can we find her?" Becca's voice was peppered with a dash of irritation. Colby raised his brow ever so slightly, encouraging her to keep her cool. They didn't need to antagonize Mr. Trotter, especially when he seemed willing to share information.

Trotter pointed to a small house sitting on the corner. "Sally's home is there, but today she went with her son and daughter-in-law to Siesta Key. They fish or walk along the sand, and she sits and watches the people."

Colby groaned internally. "How far away would that be?"

The big man pursed his lips and shrugged. "Too far to go by bike."

"I have a car."

"Then you will have no problem." Trotter pointed west.

"Siesta Beach is eight miles away on the Gulf. Follow the signs along the highway."

"Where will we find Sally?"

"Sitting under a large orange beach umbrella."

"She's Amish?" Becca asked.

"Sally is a friend of the Amish and Mennonite communities, but she's *English*."

Colby and Becca offered their thanks and headed back to the car, encouraged by having a name and a possible contact who might know about the Yoder brothers. In spite of the afternoon traffic, they soon arrived at the beach.

Colby parked in the lot provided and sat for a long moment as Becca took in the view of the peaceful inlet on the far western side of the city. The white sandy beach eased into crystal-blue water that stretched to the horizon. Gulls circled overhead, and an occasional pelican glided over the waves seemingly oblivious to the scattering of people on the shore.

"Such a beautiful spot." Becca inhaled deeply. "The air's clean, fresher than anything I've ever smelled."

"You sound like my sisters."

"Is that a bad thing?"

He regarded her sweet face, feeling a strong desire to draw her close. In truth Becca didn't remind him of his sisters. She reminded him of all that was good in life. Unable to stop himself, he reached for a lock of her hair.

She turned to face him, her gaze full of question.

"I'm glad you transferred to Georgia, Becca. Meeting you has helped me put some of the pieces of my past in better focus."

"Is that a good thing, Colby?" Her voice low and full of emotion.

He touched her cheek. "Why wouldn't it be?"

"I've spent eight years running from my past."

"I'll help you find Jacob."

She smiled. "Let's see if we can find Sally first."

Pulling back, Colby realized, once again, that he needed to be cautious around Becca and not reveal the mix of feelings that welled up within him whenever they were together.

He pointed toward the beach. "Notice the orange beach umbrella."

Becca nodded. "Looks like we've found her. Let's hope she'll lead us to at least one of the Yoder brothers."

Sally Schrock was petite and wrinkled with bright pink lipstick and rosy cheeks, not from the sun but from makeup. Her flamboyant beach cover-up and painted nails didn't match the Amish and Mennonite profile of the other folks they'd met in Pinecraft, but if what Trotter had told them was true, she knew the people and fit in with the vacating tourists.

"Mr. Trotter said we'd find you here," Becca mentioned once she had introduced herself and Colby.

A couple of rods and reels were stuck in the sand. An insulated cooler sat nearby. Sally pointed to two empty beach chairs.

"The fish aren't biting today. My daughter and son-in-law are taking a long walk. You might as well sit down and tell me what you need to know."

Without delving into what had happened at Fort Rickman or in Harmony, Becca recounted their trip south and desire to learn more about Jacob and Ezekiel Yoder.

"They were good boys," Sally said with a nod of her bleached hair. "They worked hard and obeyed their mother, although Mrs. Yoder was a hard taskmaster."

"Mrs. Yoder?" Colby shifted forward in his chair.

"That's right. Her husband left her when the boys were young. She ran the business and kept the boys on a tight schedule. They were helping her at an early age and worked far harder than I thought was acceptable."

Sally shrugged her slender shoulders. "In those days, we

didn't have the Department of Children and Family Services to call."

"Was abuse involved?" Becca asked.

"Not overt. But the boys were never allowed to play with the other children. They attended public school, but she frequently kept them home from school to help out, especially in the winter snowbird season."

"Didn't the school realize what was happening?"

"I called the principal a few times. She said if the boys were not physically hurt there was nothing she could do."

"What type of business did Mrs. Yoder have?"

"A bakery and coffee shop. Not too large, but she had a lot of return customers. She kept her staff at a minimum, and as the boys grew they took on more of the workload."

"Did you know the boys?"

"Only from the bakery. Ezekiel was younger than Jacob. Both of them left town years ago."

"And Mrs. Yoder?" Becca asked.

"That's the sad part. She opened the bakery each morning at five. The boys would follow a short while later after they did their chores at home."

Becca looked at Colby as if anticipating what Sally would say next.

"One winter morning there was a terrible explosion. My house was blocks away, and I thought it was either an earthquake or a bomb. Then I heard the sirens from the fire department and paramedics."

Sally shook her head, her eyes filled with regret. "Mrs. Yoder was trapped in the bakery and didn't survive."

"Did they determine the cause?"

"A gas leak. When Mrs. Yoder turned on the stove, the place blew. Her customers were devastated. The boys were less obvious with their grieving. They moved in with a neighbor family for a while and eventually headed north."

"What about Jacob?" Becca asked. "Do you know where he went?"

Sally shook her head. "He left Pinecraft before his brother and never came back. The neighbor said losing his mother was too much for Jacob to bear. Evidently he'd loved her, although I don't see how he could have endured her hateful words and cruel verbal attacks."

"Did he ever strike back at her?"

The older woman shook her head. "He was quiet around her as if he didn't want to draw her attention, but…"

"What, Sally?"

"I saw him look at her sometimes when he didn't know I was watching. He'd narrow his gaze and fist his hands. Both boys ran from her when she went into a rage. I'm sure they suffered when she found them. Since Jacob was older, I often wondered if he didn't try to protect his brother."

"And took the blows for both of them?" Becca asked.

Sally shrugged. "That's what I always thought. Jacob never shed a tear at her funeral, but I couldn't blame him as vengeful as that woman had been."

"Did you ever see Jacob again?"

"Never."

"What about the neighbors who took them in?"

"They left town some years back."

"And Ezekiel? Can you provide a description of him?"

Sally nodded. "Both boys were similar in height and build. Same dark hair. Ezekiel wasn't as handsome, and the difference was noticeable."

"Did people mistake one brother for the other," Becca asked.

"Never."

ELEVEN

After leaving the beach, Becca and Colby stopped at the local police department and talked to a few of the officers who remembered the explosion that had claimed Mrs. Yoder's life. According to their recollection, the blast had been accidental and caused by a faulty stove.

Both special agents left business cards with contact information and asked the officers to call them if they recalled any additional information.

"We'll have to stop overnight along the way," Colby told Becca once they were back on the interstate, heading north to Georgia.

She raised her cell phone. "I'll call ahead and see if I can find accommodations."

Becca reserved two rooms at the Florida Rest Motel about ninety miles outside of Sarasota. When they checked in, she was given a ground-floor room at the side of the complex. Colby parked nearby and ensured she was inside before he climbed the stairs to his own room. Once he stashed his overnight bag, he retraced his steps and knocked on her door.

"It's Colby." He tapped again.

When she failed to answer, he glanced at the parking lot and the densely wooded area beyond. Surely nothing had happened in such a short time. He knocked again and then hustled along the sidewalk to the front of the motel. Entering the lobby, he let out a sigh of relief.

Becca was talking to the man behind the check-in counter. "Breakfast is at 6:00 a.m., ma'am. It's served here in the café." He pointed to a room filled with small tables.

She thanked the clerk and turned toward the door. Her

brow lifted, and a lopsided smile tugged at her lips when she spied Colby. "Is something wrong?"

He shook his head a little too quickly and tried to calm his racing heart. "No, of course not. Just checking out the facilities."

"The workout room is down the hall. The motel offers a continental breakfast that starts at six. What time do you want to get started in the morning? I'd like thirty minutes in the gym, if we have time."

"Sure, no problem. Just call me when you're ready to leave." He hesitated then added, "Working out on the treadmill might be a good idea. Shall we meet up at five-thirty for PT.?"

"Perfect." She patted his arm and walked around him. "See you in the morning."

"May I help you, sir?" the clerk asked.

"Coffee for my room?"

"Certainly." He reached under the counter and pulled out two sealed foil packets. "Anything else, sir?"

"A place to grab some food?"

"There's fast food out the door and to the left. For more formal dining, you'll have to drive about five miles."

"Fast food works. Thanks."

He exited the lobby and walked around the perimeter of the motel, scouting out the entire complex. One of the first tenets of military readiness was to know the terrain. The motel was a square structure surrounded on all sides by a parking lot. Beyond the pavement in the rear, he spied a field of orange trees. A single-lane dirt road allowed access for farm vehicles.

He stared long and hard into the falling darkness. Satisfied no one was lying in wait, he walked across the parking lot to the small restaurant. After ordering two combo burgers with fries and drinks and a chicken sandwich, he hurried back to the motel, bypassed the stairway to the second floor and stopped outside Becca's door.

"It's Colby," he said as he knocked.

The curtain pulled back, and she peered out the window.

He lifted the bag of food. "I brought chow."

The lock turned and the door opened.

"I thought you might be hungry," he said to Becca, who stood in the doorway.

Her eyes danced from the bag to his face and to the bag again. "Actually, food sounds great. Come in."

He placed the bag on the round table by the window and settled into one of the two barrel chairs. "Burger and fries or a chicken sandwich?"

"The burger works for me, but what about you?"

"I ordered two, just in case. I'll save the chicken for dessert."

She smiled and opened the disposable container he handed her. "As much as I ate at lunch, I shouldn't be hungry."

He lowered his head in prayer.

"Oh, sorry." She dropped her hands to her lap and glanced down. Both of them looked up a few seconds later. She smiled apologetically. "I've gotten out of the habit."

He nodded, understanding. "I was just following Dawson's lead yesterday. He got me thinking about where God was in my life." Colby took a bite of the burger and grabbed a handful of fries.

"And?" she asked, once he came up for air.

He raised his brow. "Pardon?"

"And where is God in your life?"

He pointed toward the ceiling. "Up there someplace."

With a laugh, he added, "I don't mean the second floor. He's reigning over the world, taking care of business."

She tilted her head, her eyes inquiring. "Are we part of his business?"

"What do you think?"

She took a sip of her drink before she answered. "I used to think God cared. That what I did was important to Him. Then I grew up and things got more complicated. My struggle with my own *datt* influenced the way I thought about God the Father."

She wiped a few crumbs off the table. "Seems when I turned my back on one, I turned my back on the other as well. Since then I've been on my own."

"But you still believe in God?" he asked.

"I know He's out there." She extended her hand and then pointed at the ceiling just as Colby had done. "Maybe I should say 'up there' as you mentioned, but He's busy with big issues that are more important than my life."

"Is that what your father told you?"

She tilted her head and stared at him. "Why do you ask?"

"Just something that came to mind. Maybe it's the tone you use when you talk about your dad. I got the idea he was a strict authoritarian. When he said something you were expected to obey."

"He said I shouldn't tax God's patience and should accept my life as it was."

"Evidently, he wasn't a touchy-feely type of guy."

She smiled at his sarcasm. "To say the least."

"The way I see it—" Colby wiped his mouth and then dropped the napkin in his lap "—Christ is always ready to help us through the hard times, but we have to ask for His help. We need to invite Him into our lives because of free will. The choice is ours to accept His help or reject it."

Becca frowned. "Are there only two options?"

"Far as I can figure, that's it. If you're not inviting Him into your life, then you've got a keep-out sign on your soul. Because of free will, He won't barge in."

"Which way are you going?"

"I'm ready to open the door I closed in Afghanistan."

She watched him with questioning eyes as if waiting for Colby to reveal more. No reason to mention Ellen—an independent woman who had stolen his heart and then discarded it because of her own need for independence. Better to keep the past in the past.

Thankfully, Becca didn't press the point.

She finished the burger and threw the cardboard container in the trash. Colby tidied his side of the table.

"You didn't eat the chicken sandwich," she said when he stood.

"I'll save it for later."

She reached for her purse. "How much do I owe you?"

"Not a problem." At times Becca seemed as independent as Ellen. Maybe more so.

She pulled out a twenty and handed it to him. "You bought lunch today. I'll spring for dinner."

"Keep your money."

Evidently what he had been feeling about their relationship was lost on Becca. She considered him just another special agent with whom she was assigned to work. Why had he thought a deeper bond had developed between them, something more personal, more intimate?

Frustrated, he threw the bag in the trash.

"What about the chicken sandwich?" she asked.

"I'm not hungry anymore." He reached for the door. "Call me when you're ready to leave in the morning."

Colby flexed his muscles and inhaled a lungful of cool night air when he left her room, relieved to be away from the confused look that had wrapped around her pretty face.

She didn't have a clue about the way he felt, although at the present moment, he was as mixed-up as she looked. On the one hand, he knew Becca was a fellow agent and their relationship needed to be professional and not personal.

The problem remained that, for all her determination, Becca had a vulnerability that touched him to the core. In his family, women were cherished, including his five sisters who drove him crazy when they ganged up on him.

His father adored their mother. She was a strong woman, yet she allowed her husband to care for her in a million small ways that showed his love.

Colby had learned from his dad through observation, but also from the man-to-man talks they'd had on a regular basis since he'd been old enough to realize he was outnumbered by girls in the Voss family.

So why couldn't he buy Becca a burger, insignificant though that might be?

He sighed and shook his head. Time for a reality check. Shove the emotion aside and get back to the job at hand.

His elbow grazed against the weapon on his hip. He stopped at the stairwell and glanced around the parking area, feeling an immediate sense of unease. The last of his frustration dissipated, replaced by an alertness that signaled danger.

A few cars drove along the main road in front of the motel. He glanced at the grove of orange trees behind the lodging. Sweeping his gaze forward, he searched the dark, wooded area, looking for movement. He tilted his head and listened for the sound of footsteps or the crunch of broken glass and breathed in deeply, checking for smoke or anything out of the norm that could be the reason for his internal agitation.

Once again, he walked the perimeter of the motel, especially aware of the thick wooded areas, and stopped frequently to listen and stare into the night.

The overhead lights on the fast-food restaurant flicked off. A lone clerk, visible through the large glass windows, grabbed his jacket and left through a side door. The kid checked the lock before hurrying to his car.

Colby watched him pull onto the main highway, heading

south. The hum of his engine eventually died, leaving only the sound of cicadas and tree frogs to fill the void.

Convinced his internal alert system was being too sensitive in this peaceful, rural setting, Colby returned to the stairwell. He glanced quickly at Becca's door and the glow of light behind the pulled curtains, before he climbed to the second floor and entered his own room. He opened the drapes and stood in the darkness, staring down at the parking lot below.

What had caused his warning signal to go on high alert? Was it being with Becca this evening and getting upset about her need to pull her own weight that had made him tilt off center?

Or was danger lurking outside? Something or someone waiting for Colby to lower his guard?

Becca may think she could take care of herself, but if Jacob Yoder or someone else planned to harm her, she needed to be careful and cautious, which was exactly why Colby planned to remain vigilant throughout the night.

Becca sat on her bed fully clothed and checked the local news on her smart phone. Two men had been shot in a nearby town after trying to rob a convenience store. The owner kept a gun under the counter and, to his credit, had been able to defend himself and his store.

Squinting from the glare of light, she clicked off the bedside lamp to better view the touch screen on her phone. Although the room was dark, she could see the outline of her own service revolver on the nightstand and remembered back to the first gun-safety classes she'd had in basic training. In spite of her pacifist upbringing, learning to shoot and maintain her weapon had brought peace of mind, knowing if Jacob found her, she could protect herself.

Yet the weapon had offered little protection from the gas

explosion. What had prompted her to go into the kitchen for a glass of water? Had God been watching out for her?

With her history, the Lord's involvement seemed unlikely, yet wasn't that what Colby had been trying to say? God was always ready to intervene, when and if we turned to Him in our need. Had she called out to God that night, even subconsciously, and asked His help?

The thought of what could have happened made her stomach tighten. She glanced at the closed motel drapes and the locked door. Strong as she tried to be, she had to be aware of her surroundings at all times.

She didn't have the luxury of relying on someone else to keep her safe. Maybe because she had never had anyone who stepped into that protective role, which Colby seemed so willing to take on.

Yet, she couldn't rely on him. If she did, she might let down her guard, and that could prove deadly.

Better to ensure she kept a barrier up between them. She shook her head and sighed, regretting the reality of her life and wishing that she and Colby could have met under different circumstances.

For a moment she lost herself, thinking of his dark eyes and square jaw and the strength of his arms when he'd saved her life in Alabama. She remembered the masculine scent of his aftershave and the way his breath had fanned her neck.

Memories of his closeness weren't helping her stay strong. In fact, they were confusing her even more. Determined to get her mind off Colby, she dropped her legs to the side of the bed. Time to change into her sweats and call it a night. Morning would come too early.

Before she could place her phone on the nearby table, a shuffle sounded on the walkway outside her room.

A footstep perhaps?

Her heart pounded a warning. She tilted her head toward the window and waited for the sound to come again.

There it was.

A footfall as if someone was walking ever so quietly toward her room.

She freed her weapon from its holster. With the phone in her other hand, she slowly and deliberately moved to the opposite side of the room and stood with her back to the wall and her gun aimed at the door.

Again she listened.

A twig snapped near the window.

Too close.

She tapped Colby's number into her cell. As soon as she hit Send, a barrage of gunfire broke the silence. The window exploded and shards of glass showered over the bed where she had sat moments earlier.

Becca flattened herself against the wall. Bullets cut through the bedding and mattress.

A pause—not more than a second or two—before another stream of shots ate through the motel door. Wood fragments flew in the air like confetti. A sharp chip cut into her cheek.

Her ears roared from the explosive bursts.

As quick as it started, it was over. Footfalls pounded the pavement, running away from the motel.

She threw open the shattered door.

A dark form sprinted across the parking lot toward the densely forested area beyond. "Halt!" she screamed, her weapon aimed at the fleeing shooter.

A car turned into the parking lot, blocking her line of fire.

"Stop," she yelled at the driver and held up her hand. "Stay in your car."

She raced around the vehicle and chased after the assailant, pushing her legs to go faster.

He turned and looked back.

She couldn't see his face in the darkness, but she saw a flash from his weapon.

A lightning bolt of fire grazed her left arm.

Gasping at the pain, she nearly stumbled.

The guy was tall with broad shoulders.

Jacob?

He ran toward the woods.

She stopped, raised her weapon and fired. One shot. Then another.

He slipped between the trees.

Footsteps sounded behind her.

She glanced over her shoulder.

Colby.

"He went into the woods," she called to him. "Circle to the right. We'll block his exit."

Becca ran until she came to a roadway. In the distance, a car turned onto the main highway.

She plugged 911 into her phone and notified the operator to contact the local police to be on the lookout for a car headed south.

"A dark sedan. No, I can't identify the make or model." She gasped, needing to catch her breath. "I'm at the Florida Rest Motel. The attacker fired repeatedly into my motel room."

Colby approached her. "Did we lose him?"

"He drove off." She pointed to the road then gave her name and room number to the operator.

"What happened?" Colby asked when she disconnected.

She filled him in with halting breaths.

Colby reached tenderly for her arm. "You're hit."

"It's not bad. A graze. That's all."

"You could have been killed."

Becca paused, realizing what he had said was true. "But I'm okay." She needed to reassure him as well as herself. "I heard sounds outside my room and grabbed my weapon. Before I could open my door, the window shattered."

He stepped closer and touched her cheek. "Your face is bleeding."

"From a sliver of wood."

Sirens sounded in the distance.

Colby's voice caught. "I wanted to keep you safe, but I wasn't there when you needed me."

She could have used his help, and maybe together, they would have captured Jacob. But what she needed to hear more than anything was the tenderness in Colby's voice. She'd been hiding from Jacob for too long and not allowing anyone to get close. All that had changed when she transferred to Fort Rickman and met Colby.

He'd been the first man to break through her defenses. Being with him made her realize there was more to life than living in constant fear.

She couldn't tell him the truth. Instead, she tried to shove her armor back in place, only the adrenaline rush ended just that quickly, sapping her energy and leaving her shaking and gasping for air.

A lump filled her throat. Colby was right. She could have been killed.

He opened his arms, and she collapsed into his embrace. Tears burned her eyes.

"Shhh," he soothed.

Wrapped in the cocoon of his protectiveness, she let Colby lead her through the darkness. She inhaled the manly smell of him and heard his heart beating in his chest. His strength buoyed her weakness, and more than anything, she wanted to hold on to him and never let him go.

He kissed her forehead and sent a volley of emotion rambling through her. As much as she tried to ignore the longing, she wanted him to kiss her lips and pull her even more tightly into his embrace.

The bright strobe lights of the law enforcement vehicle captured both of them as they stepped into the glare of light.

Becca straightened and swiped her hand across her cheeks. As much as she wanted to stay wrapped in Colby's embrace she needed to be realistic. This was her fight and her family that needed to be avenged.

She couldn't rely on Colby to always help her. If Jacob came after her again, she'd do what she should have done years ago, and that was to confront Jacob face-to-face.

Colby couldn't get past the memory of holding Becca in his arms. Feeling her mold into his embrace had sent an explosion of sensations through his body. Even now, he was having trouble getting his emotions under control.

Seeing her hurt had nearly torn him in two. The EMTs had quickly assured him both injuries were superficial and would heal without complication, however he still stood close, with a watchful eye, as they cleaned the cut on her face and bandaged her arm.

"The paramedic said you need to take it easy for the next twenty-four hours," he told Becca when the medical team returned to their vehicle.

"I'll rest while you drive us home," she assured him.

After they provided information to the local law enforcement, Colby checked them out of the motel and helped her into the car.

"Shall I adjust the seat belt?" he asked.

She smiled sweetly and patted his hand. "Thank you for your concern, but I'm more worried about you having to drive back to Georgia after the stressful night."

With fewer cars on the road at this time of night, the miles passed quickly. Becca stared at the flickering lights and rested her head against the seat.

"Where'd he go, Colby?" she mused.

"Jacob?" Colby flicked his gaze at her.

She nodded.

"He went back to wherever he's been holed up all these years, like a fox in his lair."

"Eight years." She shook her head. "There's no record of

his whereabouts. I've checked repeatedly and could never find any thread that led back to him. He must have lived off the land or off the good-heartedness of the Amish since he didn't leave a social security trail. No credit cards or phone or cell phone records to confirm he was alive during all that time. Tracking him down could be impossible, unless—"

She picked up her phone and touched a number of apps.

"What are you looking for?" Colby asked.

"The locations of other Amish communities."

"You can't access all of them, Becca. They're spread out around the country."

"But I can focus on the ones closest to Alabama and Georgia."

"You can't call them or send a text." Colby stated the obvious, but he was trying to be realistic.

"I'll call law enforcement in nearby municipalities and small towns and inquire about crime in the area, especially fires or gas explosions that led to loss of life."

Colby realized where she was going. "And any widows who may have been hoodwinked by an Amish drifter."

"Exactly. Jacob came to Harmony from somewhere. He posed as a drifter who hired out to the widow he eventually married. That's probably the way he's been operating all this time and keeping under the radar. He hits on some unassuming older woman who needs help and then bilks her out of her money or land or both."

"Did you know the woman he married in Harmony?"

Becca nodded. "Mary was a nice lady but rather sickly. Her husband had died of a heart attack. Both her house and land fell into disrepair. Other men in the community helped out when they could, but they had their own farms to tend. Everyone feared she'd lose her property, although a real estate agent claimed a buyer was interested."

"Was Jacob part of the community at that time?"

"He showed up soon thereafter. Easy enough for him to

see there was a problem with the neglected farm." Becca brushed a strand of hair back from her face. "He'd done the same thing at our farm. In fact, that's how I met him. He knocked at the door looking for work."

"Because your home needed repair?"

She nodded. "Although that's an understatement. My father would have loved having Jacob's help, but he didn't have money for any hired hands. *Datt* offered him lodging in the barn, which he accepted for a few weeks. Before long, he was helping the widow. Eventually, he proposed and moved in with her."

"Jacob was younger than Mary?" Colby asked.

"Much younger, but even with the Amish such things happen. Jacob had a way of charming people, including the elders. They were happy the widow was being cared for."

"Did Jacob know about the offer on the land?"

"I'm not sure. I never heard him mention selling the farm."

"When did you start working for him?"

"Not long after he and Mary had married. Her heath had declined. Jacob needed help with the house so he contacted my father. Much as I didn't want to work for Jacob, my *datt* insisted."

"What was Jacob like?" Colby asked.

"He could turn on a dime. He had seemed nice when I first met him, but he changed. Or perhaps he had been hiding his true self all along. I soon noticed how he treated his wife when he didn't think I was watching."

"Did you mention your concerns to your father?"

"Not at first. I knew he would say the problem was with me and not Jacob. That's exactly what happened when I finally told him how worried I was about Mary's health."

"Worried in what way?"

"She kept growing weaker. I suspected Jacob was giving her something to hasten her debilitation."

"Poison?"

Becca sighed. "Perhaps. I had no proof, but he wouldn't allow her to see a doctor, and she often grew more agitated when he was around. I never saw any signs of physical abuse, but I overheard him belittle her on more than one occasion."

"Was that the reason you finally talked to your dad?"

Becca rubbed her forehead and didn't speak for a long moment.

"Do you feel okay?" he asked.

"A headache, that's all."

"You need to rest, Becca. Too much has happened. You should talk to Wilson. Tell him to take you off the case. He'll understand."

She shook her head. "I'm the perfect person to go after Jacob. I know what he looks like, the sound of his voice. He can walk in both the *English* world and the plain without being questioned, yet an Amish community is the perfect place for him to hide out because the people stick to themselves and don't mix with the locals in nearby towns. He's hidden with their help for too long."

"Just as long as we work together, Becca."

"I called you tonight, Colby, when I heard someone outside my room. You didn't answer."

She was right. He had seen the record of her call on his smart phone, but he hadn't heard it ring because he'd been on the far side of the building rechecking the perimeter of the motel as a security precaution.

What he had heard was the gunfire, but he'd arrived at Becca's room too late. Seeing the broken window and battered door had sent his heart to his throat until he'd spied her running into the woods.

He had wanted to keep Becca safe, but he hadn't been there in time.

He wouldn't let it happen again. He was committed to protecting Becca and bringing Jacob Yoder to justice.

TWELVE

Becca and Colby arrived on post in time for her to grab a few hours of sleep before her alarm went off the next morning. The night before, Colby had insisted on escorting her inside and then checked her room before he finally said good-night.

She could get used to having Colby around. Not that she couldn't handle things on her own, but an extra set of eyes working an investigation was nice, especially on a difficult case. Besides, bouncing ideas back and forth helped her sort through the fragments of information they had already gleaned.

Something else was nice about Colby. He had a funny way of touching her arm when he was concerned about her well-being. She tried to ignore the warmth that flowed though her whenever he was near and instead blamed her fluctuating internal temperature on the weather. But southern Georgia's temps were hovering around forty degrees at night with daytime highs in the mid-fifties.

The truth was that Colby's closeness affected her internal thermostat because she was attracted to the handsome agent. Although she knew better than to allow attraction to get in the way of an investigation, she couldn't help herself. At least Colby didn't realize the effect he had on her. She needed to keep her emotions in check as long as possible. Colby was her partner professionally, but not in any other way.

End of story.

In spite of the post-wide training holiday, a number of folks were at their desks when she entered CID Headquarters that morning.

Raynard Otis saluted and then offered her a welcoming

smile. "How's it going, Agent Miller?" he asked when she stopped in front of his desk.

"You should be home relaxing, Ray. Didn't you get the memo about the training holiday?"

"Yes, ma'am, and no, ma'am. I read the memo, but where else would I want to be this morning?" He shrugged. His mocha face stretched into a wide grin. "Everyone else came to work today. We've got a major investigation plus other time-sensitive directives that I need to take over to post headquarters. By the way, Chief Wilson said you might be interested in working on the farmers' market task force the general's wife is leading."

Becca held up her hand and shook her head. "Not until we get to the bottom of this current investigation. Is the chief in his office?"

"No, ma'am. I expect he'll arrive shortly."

Becca stopped momentarily at the coffeepot to pour a cup before heading to her office. A bare desk greeted her. No flowers. No plants. No photos of family. Just a computer and a stack of manila folders.

Nice and neat, the way she liked her life to be.

Except things had suddenly gotten complicated.

Logging in to her computer, she quickly produced a list of Amish communities and corresponding law enforcement agencies in the nearby towns. She printed off two copies.

Becca heard Colby's voice before she saw him. He greeted Ray and took the same path she had earlier to the break room and the coffeepot. In spite of the caffeine, he looked tired when he entered her cubicle some minutes later.

"Long time no see." His dark eyes twinkled, and his lips pulled into a smile.

"Did you sleep at all?" she asked.

"A few hours. And you?"

"The same."

"How's the arm?" he asked.

She glanced down at the bandage. "It's fine."

"You always say you're fine. Sometimes I wish you'd let me in on your life."

She stared at him for a long moment. "Okay." Her right hand rubbed across the bandage. "It's sore, but no significant pain."

He nodded. "That's better. Now let's talk to the chief."

"He's not here yet. I checked on the way in."

Colby pointed to her computer. "I can contact some of those law enforcement agencies near Amish communities, if you've got a list handy."

"I'd appreciate the help." She handed a copy of the list to Colby. "If you work from the top down, I'll start at the bottom."

"You know where to find me." He took the printout she offered and waved as he left her cubicle.

The work was slow and frustrating. Becca's optimism plummeted as one after another of the law enforcement agencies had little or no information about crime within the Amish communities, especially nothing about widows dying in explosions or house fires.

Becca rubbed her neck to stave off stiffness from wedging the phone between her shoulder and ear for too long and was glad for the interruption when Colby tapped his knuckles on the wall to her cubicle and peered inside.

"The chief arrived a few minutes ago. Brody is debriefing him now about Arnold. We're scheduled next."

"Let me make one more phone call."

He nodded. "See you in ten minutes."

She plugged in the next number on her list and asked to speak to the chief of police of a small town in Eastern Tennessee once someone answered.

"This is Chief O'Brian." A deep voice.

She pulled the phone closer to her ear.

"Chief, this is Special Agent Becca Miller. I'm with the

U.S. Army Criminal Investigation Division at Fort Rickman, Georgia."

"Thanks for your service, and God bless the military. What can I do for you, Agent Miller?"

She provided a brief but accurate description of what had happened in Harmony eight years ago and the need to determine where Jacob Yoder had been living since that time. "We think he may have killed one of our construction contractors on post."

The chief clucked his tongue while Becca waited, hoping for some small bit of information that could help her track down Jacob.

"I don't recall anyone named Yoder," the chief replied. "We did have a guy, about two years ago, by the name of Lapp. Jacob Lapp. Sounds like a similar M.O."

"How's that?"

"Lapp appeared one day and starts helping one of the Amish widows with a farm in need of a man to run it. They marry, her health declines and she dies some months later. No one was suspicious until he wiped out her bank account and skipped town before we could bring him in for questioning."

"Do you happen to have a description?"

"Give me a minute to find the file."

Becca tapped her fingers on her desk.

"Here you go." The cop's voice. "Lapp was six-two. Dark hair. Small scar on his left cheek."

Becca wanted to clap her hands with glee. "That sounds like my perp. When was the last time you saw him?"

"The day of his wife's funeral. He hasn't been seen since then."

She thanked the man, disconnected and with smooth strokes wrote the information on a tablet of paper. She pushed her chair back and hurried to find Colby.

"I've got something." She held up the pad.

"Tell me as we head to the chief's office."

"A chief of police in eastern Tennessee has seen our guy. Same type of deal. An Amish widow. Failing health. She died and Jacob—this time going by the name Jacob Lapp—walked away with her money."

"How long ago did she die?"

"Two years."

"That doesn't prove it was Yoder, Becca."

"The description fits."

"A big Amish guy with dark hair. How many men could fill that description?"

Colby was right, but it was the only lead they'd had so far, and Becca wasn't ready to dismiss the information as insignificant. If Lapp was Yoder, then Jacob was still alive.

In spite of her earlier euphoria, she knew that without an eyewitness or fingerprints or DNA nothing could establish that the two men were the same. Even a photo would be a plus. But all Becca knew was a man named Lapp had lost his wife and moved on with the money that was rightfully his through marriage.

No crime. No evidence. No proof she could place on Wilson's desk. She'd be better off to keep the information to herself until she had something more significant to report.

She needed to make a good impression on Wilson, but at this point, she didn't know where she stood. Working with Colby added another complication to a very difficult case.

Colby tapped on the chief's door. "Sir, do you have a minute?"

Wilson glanced at his watch and then motioned for Colby and Becca to enter. "I have to be at the commanding general's office in twenty minutes. What do you have?"

"A possible suspect in the Arnold murder, sir." Aware of the time constraint, Colby gave the chief a brief overview of what they'd learned about Jacob and his brother and concluded with mention of the shooting at the motel.

"Did you receive medical treatment when you returned to post, Becca?" Wilson asked.

She shook her head. "It wasn't necessary, sir. The Florida EMTs cleaned and bandaged the wound last night. It's a superficial graze and should heal without additional medical attention."

"You might want to go on sick call and see if the doc thinks an antibiotic would be helpful. I don't want an infection to set it."

"I'll watch for any warning signs."

Wilson seemed satisfied. He pursed his lips and steepled his fingers, elbows perched on his desk. "I have a problem considering Jacob Yoder as the attacker last night or the person who murdered Arnold. From what you said, Yoder was killed in a house fire in Harmony." The chief pushed back in his chair and spread his hands across his desk. "I don't see how he could have committed this crime."

Colby had thought the same thing himself early on. Now, after everything that had happened, he believed Jacob was a very likely suspect.

"Sir, Becca believes the man killed in the house fire was Yoder's brother," Colby offered. "The two men were of similar stature and appearance. A mistaken identification seems probable."

Wilson looked at Becca. "Does the Harmony sheriff share your suspicions?"

She shook her head. "I don't think so, sir."

"Was DNA testing done before interment?"

"No, sir."

"Are they willing to exhume the body to make a more definitive identification?"

"Not that I know of."

He glanced at Colby, then back at Becca. "I'm more prone

to consider the Macon connection as significant in this investigation. Brody came across the owner of a small company whose bid on the housing contract for the new BOQs wasn't accepted. He's had some brushes with the law and has been known to retaliate when his company's offer wasn't accepted. He sent one competitor to the hospital with broken ribs and a cracked jaw. Brody can fill you in."

"Yes, sir."

"If you turn up any concrete evidence that Jacob Yoder is alive, let me know, and we can reevaluate. As it stands now, going after a dead man seems a waste of time and effort."

"What about the shooting last night, sir?" Becca pressed.

"Anyone have a grudge against you?"

"Yes, sir. Jacob Yoder."

Wilson steeled his jaw. From all appearances, he didn't like her rather flip response. "Maybe you should back off a bit, Agent Miller."

Becca frowned. "I'm not sure what you mean, sir."

"What I mean is stay on post and keep a low profile. I want you to handle the security for the farmers' market and craft fair. I've submitted your name to Mrs. Cameron."

"But—"

The chief cut her off and pointed to Colby. "Let Agent Voss do the legwork on the investigation. You can help him here in the office. I don't want you placed in danger. The CID was short-staffed for too long. Now that I've got a few new faces in the office, I want to keep everyone healthy and productive."

He opened a folder. "Do you know anyone named Brad Nicholson?"

She hesitated as if trying to place the name. "No one comes to mind, sir."

"He's the Macon contractor. I just wanted to ensure both sides of the investigation aren't looking at the same person."

"Sir, Jacob Yoder killed my father and sister. He vowed to kill me."

Wilson's eyes narrowed. "That's significant for sure. But the fact that Yoder is dead seems to close that part of the investigation. Do you understand, Becca?"

"Yes, sir."

Only the look on her face told Colby that she didn't understand nor did she go along with the chief's assessment of the situation or his guidance about her staying out of the line of fire. From what he already knew about Becca, staying at the office wasn't how she wanted to handle this investigation.

Would she obey Wilson's directives. Or would she continue to look for a dead man that she feared was very much alive?

Becca wanted to pound her fist against her desk. She was frustrated with Wilson. Had he even listened to what she told him?

Her father hadn't listened when she revealed the truth about Jacob. Now Wilson was focusing on other clues and missing the very real killer that Becca knew was in the local area.

The chief might think she'd be safe on post, but Jacob seemed able to slip through on-post security with ease. The man needed to be flushed out of hiding, which meant finding him before he found her. Becca wouldn't let him get away. Not this time.

"Come with me," she said to Colby once he entered her cubical.

"You heard the chief, Becca. He wants you to stay on post. Don't go hunting for trouble."

"He's sending Brody on a wild-goose chase. That Macon contractor sounds like a puffed-up marshmallow compared to Jacob."

"Wilson's thinking of your own good, Becca."

"What about the next widow Jacob targets? He's got devious methods that have worked for him in the past. Why wouldn't he be hiding in plain sight in the nearby community? We need to find out who lives in that house in the clearing."

Colby nodded. "I agree, but—"

"Then we're on the same page. By the way, I sent the photos of the car in the barn to forensics, along with the photo of the marks we saw on the side of the road after the shooting in Alabama." She picked up her phone and opened the photo file. "Look at these tire tracks."

He studied the photo, then pulled out his own phone and clicked on his file. He put the photo of the tracks he'd taken in Alabama next to the tracks Becca had photographed in the barn.

"The clarity isn't sharp enough, but both tracks could have been made by the same tires."

She nodded. "And the same vehicle. Let's take a little ride into the country."

"Becca," Colby warned.

"We're not investigating. We're merely seeing the countryside."

"Wilson told you to stay put."

"And before that, he said for us to work together. You told me we're partners."

"Things have changed since then."

She took a step back and raised her hands. "Whatever, but I'm driving to the Lodge."

"Somehow I get the feeling you'll make a detour."

She smiled. "A detour to Amish country. Come with me, Colby. Otherwise, I'll be forced to go alone."

"You're doing this against Wilson's request."

"A request," Becca restated for emphasis. "That's exactly right. The chief didn't order me to stop investigating. Rather, he encouraged me to remain safe. If you're with me, I will be safe. Besides, I'm worried about the people who live in that run-down house where we saw the car. I couldn't endure knowing my lack of action caused someone else harm."

She grabbed her keys and purse and turned toward the door. "What do you say, partner?"

Colby shook his head and sighed with frustration. "We're in this together, Becca, but you need to follow my lead. Don't do anything foolish or bold. Wilson doesn't want you hurt, and neither do I."

"Don't worry. The last thing I want is to be injured or incapacitated when I finally confront Jacob Yoder."

Colby and Becca passed the turnoff to Dawson and Lillie's house and continued on along a narrow road that eventually led to an area of Amish farmhouses. Just as before, Colby was struck by the charm of the simple life. No cars in the driveways or power and phone lines littering the landscape. Not a television dish or porch light in sight.

The land was beautiful even in its winter pause. Barren trees swayed in the wind that stirred from the west, and a flock of birds flew overhead, searching for a place to land.

Colby turned up the heat and glanced at Becca. "You should have worn a coat."

"I'm fine."

"How's the arm and don't tell me it's fine, too."

She smiled, but her eyes looked tired. "Actually, it's aching."

"You need some pain meds."

"I'll take an ibuprofen when I get back to the lodge."

"You need to go on sick call in the morning."

She nodded. "Maybe you're right."

They were definitely making progress.

"Although," she added, "I hate to seem like a weakling."

"You're not. Wouldn't you tell me the same thing if I had taken a hit?"

"You probably wouldn't listen, either."

He laughed. "You mean we're both cut from the same cloth?"

"Both CID. Both focused on getting the job done. Both type A." She paused. "Except you're the extrovert."

"And you?"

Her slender shoulders rose for a moment. "I'm usually more comfortable hanging out with myself."

She pointed to an intersection. "There's the turn."

The road wove through a dense cluster of trees before it spilled into the clearing. Colby pulled to the side of the road and killed the engine.

He studied the farmhouse. It needed a new coat of paint as if the original job had been done with a cheap product that failed to seal the wood. Curtains covered the windows. The sun peering through the cloud cover painted the house in an eerie light that was both uninviting and cold.

"We can't search without a warrant," he cautioned.

"No, but we can knock on the door and talk to whoever answers." They climbed the front steps, taking care not to trip on the loose plank.

Becca rapped boldly on the door. When no one answered, she called in a loud voice, "Is anyone home? My name's Becca Miller. I'm with the Criminal Investigation Division on Fort Rickman. I'd like to ask you a few questions."

Again she knocked, but the door remained closed.

She glanced at Colby, tilted her head and listened for any sound coming from inside the house.

"Let's check the barn," she suggested.

Colby kept glancing back at the house, feeling an ominous tightness in his shoulders as if someone was watching from behind the closed curtains.

Becca tugged on the barn door and peered inside. "The car's gone."

The two Dobermans appeared on the rise of a hill in the

distance. They were huge creatures with sleek coats and mammoth jowls.

Becca gasped.

"Back up nice and easy," Colby cautioned.

They backtracked, their eyes locked on the dogs.

Twenty feet from the car, the animals lunged forward as if on command. Their legs flew down the hillside. Their barks of protest set the hair on Colby's neck on end.

"Get in the car, Becca." He opened the door. She slipped past him.

The dogs were closing in. They bared their teeth and raced forward.

Colby slammed her door and rounded the car. He slipped behind the wheel and pulled the driver's door closed just in time. The dogs circled the car and barked ferociously. Becca shivered.

"We're safe," he said in hopes of calming her as well as his own rapid heartbeat.

He loved dogs, but not as vicious attack animals. Who owned the Dobermans? And had someone commanded them to attack?

Looking up at the window, he caught sight of a face peering around the curtain.

The Amish were a quiet people who kept to themselves, peace-loving and gentle. The vicious dogs didn't seem in keeping with their way of life. Neither did the Crown Vic they'd seen earlier in the barn.

They'd come back, but next time they'd have a search warrant so they could find whoever was hiding inside.

THIRTEEN

Becca didn't have time for a coffee klatch with the general's wife and the other folks on the committee to plan the first farmers' market and craft fair at Fort Rickman. She did, however, want to meet the bishop, who was the appointed head of the Amish community.

The following morning, Becca donned a skirt and sweater with a jacket pulled over her shoulders, and hoped she'd be suitably dressed for the meeting at Quarters One, home to every commanding general since the post was built in the 1930s.

Before the army had purchased the land, the expansive farmhouse and surrounding property had belonged to a Georgia farmer. Since then, the rambling structure had undergone a number of renovations. Painted white with large wraparound porches and a gazebo in the front yard, the home was comfortable but elegant in a simple way and befitting the commander and his wife.

Mrs. Cameron was a sweet, Southern belle who hailed from Savannah. Her accent had softened over the years of following her military husband around the world, but a trace of the South remained and seemed evident as she invited Becca into the spacious foyer.

"I'm so glad you'll be able to help us with the planning, Special Agent Miller."

"It's Becca, ma'am. Thank you for inviting me into your home."

The older woman, wearing a pretty floral dress, pointed down a hallway. "Everyone is in the family room. I had the aide build a fire, since there's a chill in the air this morning. Help yourself to coffee or tea and pastries."

"Thank you, ma'am."

A number of people from post headquarters had already arrived and were chatting among themselves when she stepped into the airy room. Decorated with aqua-and-lime-green accents, the splashes of color against the eggshell walls and neutral couches gave the room a casual feel. The logs burning in the fireplace added warmth and a homey touch that Becca found inviting.

Groupings of flowers and books and large ceramic decorative plates added to the cozy ambiance, despite the formal wainscot paneling and massive floor-to-ceiling windows.

Becca poured a cup of coffee and sat in a small chair in the corner. A middle-aged woman perched on a nearby couch stretched out her hand. "I'm Lois Simmons."

The chief of staff's wife. Becca recognized the last name and accepted the handshake. "Nice to meet you, ma'am. I'm with the CID on post."

"We haven't met before?"

"No, ma'am. I just transferred here from Germany."

"We lived in Heidelberg some years ago." The woman's eager smile revealed her appreciation of the foreign country. "I keep telling Bob we need to get assigned there again."

"It is a beautiful place."

"With wonderful people. Where were you stationed?"

"Garmisch."

"In Bavaria." Mrs. Simmons eagerly chatted about the various trips she and her husband had taken to the Black Forest and surrounding areas. "Were you there for the Passion Play in Oberammergau?"

"Unfortunately no." The three-hour performance was held every ten years and had been ongoing since 1634 in thanksgiving for God's protection over the small town during the plague.

The chief of staff's wife patted her chest with emotion. Her eyes brimmed with tears. "The reenactment of Christ's

Passion touched me deeply, especially when He was forced to carry his cross."

Becca knew about crosses, but she rarely thought about the cross Christ carried. Had she strayed so far from her faith?

Mrs. Cameron stepped into the room escorting a man, plain of dress, with a full beard. He held a hat in one hand and a small notebook and pencil in the other.

"Everyone, I'd like to introduce Bishop Isaac Zimmerman, from the Amish community. He's graciously agreed to meet with us and plan the upcoming farmers' market and craft fair that we're so excited about hosting."

She pulled up a chair and placed it on the other side of Becca.

"May I get you coffee and a pastry?" Mrs. Cameron asked the bishop.

"Thank you, yes." He smiled agreeably at the other guests. "I am pleased to join you today."

The general's wife proved to be a good facilitator, and the plans for the market and craft fair were finalized in less than two hours. Those who attended represented various organizations on post. Each group volunteered responsibility for a certain aspect of the event.

Morale Support promised a sound system for the commanding general's welcoming remarks. The post band would provide music, and the children's choirs from the Main Post Chapel would sing at various times throughout the morning.

"I'm glad Special Agent Miller could be with us today," Mrs. Cameron said, nearing the conclusion of the meeting. "Becca, you and your folks will provide security?"

"Yes, ma'am."

The bishop shook his head as if somewhat concerned. "I do not expect trouble. Do you?"

"Not at all, sir." Mrs. Cameron quickly stepped in to reassure the bishop. "But when we have so many people in an area, we like to have security on hand as a precaution. Regrettably problems sometimes occur even in the best of situations."

After a final wrap-up, Mrs. Cameron thanked the committee members for taking part in the planning task force.

As the other folks headed toward the front door, Becca stepped closer to the bishop who had placed his coffee cup and saucer on the small side table.

"Sir, I drove through the Amish community and noticed a house that sits along one of the side roads. It's surrounded by rather dense forest that opens into a clearing. The house is in need of repair, which is not in keeping with the other homes. There's a barn to the left of the main house and a hill behind. The person has two dogs, both Doberman pinschers."

The bishop nodded. "I know of this house."

"Who lives there, sir? Is it someone in your community?"

"An older woman. Fannie Lehman. Her husband died some months ago when a tree fell on him."

Just as had happened in Alabama. "I'm sorry about her loss."

The bishop nodded. "*Gott* gives life and takes it away."

"I'm sure Mrs. Lehman finds it hard to manage her land. Does she have someone to help her?"

"Why does this cause you concern?"

"I'm looking for a man who may be hiding out among the Amish. His name is Jacob Yoder. He's six-two with brown hair and a scar on his left cheek."

"I do not know this man." The bishop reached for his hat. "Besides, the Amish are peace-loving people. We do not deal with violence."

"Yet sometimes it finds you."

His eyes narrowed and his gnarly fingers gripped the brim of his hat. "You mentioned security and now you tell me of an Amish man who hides from the law. I will not take part in anything that brings discord or strife to my people.

Even if we have agreed to the market, we must maintain our way of life first. You understand, *yah?*"

A subtle warning, but one Becca understood. If she disrupted the Amish way of life, the bishop would draw back from his agreement with Fort Rickman to hold the market and craft fairs.

Mrs. Cameron stepped toward them. She glanced first at the bishop and then at Becca. "Is something wrong?"

Becca remained silent, waiting to hear what the bishop would say.

"I was discussing the Amish way with Miss Miller and our love for the peaceful life."

"Military personnel are tasked with ensuring the peace, Bishop," Becca answered. "But we know that evil people do evil things."

Turning to the general's wife, she said, "Thank you, ma'am, for the coffee. I'll see myself out."

Becca left the house frustrated by the bishop's stubborn determination to see things only his way. He didn't realize that if Jacob Yoder were in the area, the Amish could be in danger, no matter how peace-loving they were.

She climbed into her car and called Colby. "The meeting ended, and I'm headed back to CID Headquarters. Did Wilson okay the request for a search warrant?"

Colby pulled in a stiff breath. "He was hesitant and wanted to run the request past General Cameron."

Heaviness settled over Becca's shoulders as she recalled the bishop's comment. "I can guess what the general said."

"Nothing is to interfere with our good relationship with the Amish. Evidently Mrs. Cameron has been interested in getting this organized for months. The bishop was the negative force. He's only recently changed his mind."

"But what if Jacob Yoder is hiding out at the house?"

"Wilson considers that a big what-if, but to his credit, he contacted the Freemont chief of police and asked him to increase surveillance in the area. The county sheriff will provide additional backup, although without a photograph of Jacob, law enforcement doesn't know who they're looking for."

"Did you mention the scar on his cheek?"

"A lot of people have scars, Becca."

"The name of the woman who lives in the run-down house is Lehman. Fannie Lehman. Her husband died accidently a few months ago. He was killed by a fallen tree."

"Sounds familiar," Colby said.

The door to the commanding general's house opened and the bishop walked outside.

"Gotta go, Colby. I'll see you back at headquarters."

The bishop nodded goodbye to Mrs. Cameron and walked toward his buggy.

Becca stepped from her car and approached the rig.

"Bishop, I'm sorry if I caused you concern inside. I want the Amish to maintain their way of life, but there is a man I fear may cause problems. He lived in an Amish community near Harmony, Alabama. Some years ago, he killed my father and sister. He may be in this area now."

The bishop's gaze softened. "You carry great pain, and for this I am sorry, but I do not know of the man you mentioned."

"Mrs. Lehman is living alone and vulnerable. Would you ensure no one has moved in to help her? Someone who might have ulterior motives."

The bishop hesitated for a long moment and then nodded. "I will speak to her."

"Thank you, sir."

"But Ms. Miller, you mentioned an Amish community in Alabama. Your father and sister, they were plain?"

She nodded, feeling her eyes sting under his gentle scrutiny.

"And you were, as well?" he asked.

"Yah."

The bishop nodded ever so slightly. "This man, this Jacob Yoder, he caused you to flee the Amish and find safety with the *English?*"

"I was safe for eight years, but he's found me, Bishop. Now I must stop him."

"He is not Amish if he deals in violence. I will ask *Gott* to protect you so this Jacob Yoder cannot hurt you again."

He nodded farewell and climbed into the buggy, the squeak of the carriage and the slap of the reins against the horses' haunches all too familiar. The bishop clicked his tongue, and the horses stepped forward, the creak of the wheels over the pavement sounding in the morning calm.

"Remember, Becca," the bishop called back to her from the carriage. "*Gott* loves you."

"The county sheriff said he'll have his deputies patrol the Amish area," Colby said once Becca arrived back at CID Headquarters. "But he doesn't expect to find anything suspect."

"Is the Freemont chief of police interested in getting a search warrant?"

"Negative. Nor is the sheriff."

"Why not?"

"Because Jacob Yoder is dead. At least, that's what everyone believes. Don Palmer, the current chief of the local Freemont P.D., called Harmony and talked to Lewis Stone. He's sympathetic, but not willing to exhume the body."

"Which doesn't make sense."

"I called him. According to Lewis, he needs to match DNA from the exhumed remains with a DNA sample from Yoder or his brother, which he doesn't have."

Becca held up her hand. "You mean Stone needs something from Yoder's past that contains his DNA?"

"That's the problem. We don't have any leads on the

brother, and everything in Yoder's house burned to the ground."

"Is that the only thing stopping him from exhuming the body?"

"Sounds like it."

Becca nodded. "Then we'll have to dig up a sample of Jacob's DNA."

"You mean another trip to Harmony?"

She nodded. "We can go this afternoon."

"Only if you agree to the following conditions, Becca. We work together and you don't hold anything else back from me."

"I promise. Cross my heart."

As much as he wanted to ask what she had on Jacob, Colby knew Becca's reticence and decided not to press for more details. Everything would be revealed in time.

Right now, he wanted to ensure she didn't go racing off across the countryside on her own. Becca's enthusiasm to find Jacob often conflicted with her need to be cautious and vigilant.

Another concern niggled at Colby. If she had DNA evidence that led back to Jacob Yoder, there could be other secrets Becca was keeping from him, as well.

FOURTEEN

Becca sat in the passenger seat next to Colby and watched the countryside roll by as they drove back to Harmony and the Amish community. An afternoon meeting with the military police about post security had kept them tied up at the office longer than they had expected. The only plus was that Becca had been able to coordinate help for the upcoming farmers' market and craft fair following the meeting.

The traffic getting off post at the close of the workday had added to their delay. Road construction as well as a fender bender held them up even longer.

Becca glanced at the sun, low in the sky. The optimism she had felt earlier plummeted. Returning home would be hard enough in daylight. The approaching darkness made her chest tighten. The last time she had been in the house had been the middle of the night to find her sister and father slaughtered by an evil man who still wreaked havoc in too many lives.

As much as she needed to stop Jacob, she was anxious about returning to her past both figuratively and literally.

"You're quiet this evening," Colby finally said, as if aware of how deep within herself she had gone.

"You know how introverts are," she said with a half smile she didn't feel.

"Thinking about your family?"

She nodded. "And that night. Jacob had told Katie he would come after her if she tried to flee. She had struggled to keep him at a distance, but as Mary became more and more infirmed, Jacob became more brazen."

Becca tapped her fingers on the console.

"Katie feared something would happen. She called me

from Elizabeth's house." Becca's throat tightened as she heard Katie's frantic voice echo in her mind. "She said she needed me. Katie thought I could protect her and stand up to Jacob."

"You were stationed at Fort Campbell?"

"That's right. I left as fast as I could and drove nonstop for five hours. When I arrived, I found my father on the floor, the life ebbing from him. Katie had been killed in the pantry."

Looking into the darkness ahead, Becca relived the horror of that night. "I heard footsteps upstairs and knew Jacob was still in the house."

She thought again of the heavy footfalls on the stairwell as Jacob descended to the main floor. "I raced outside. Jacob stepped onto the porch and searched the night. He…"

She hesitated, unable to enter again into that moment when they had connected, his gaze finding her in the darkness. His face had contorted with rage. "He raised his hand in anger and screamed that if I ran from him, he would find me and kill me."

"You eluded him for a number of years."

"Only because I asked for assignments in Europe. I came back for a few weeks of temporary duty here and there." She pushed a strand of hair away from her face. "I…I was always looking over my shoulder, thinking Jacob was closing in on me. Even in Europe, I'd thought I'd see him in the distance. Of course, it wasn't him. It was my mind playing tricks on me."

She touched the window. "I ran out of options and talked myself into believing that he had died in the fire. The job opened at Fort Rickman. I knew Chief Wilson was a strong leader and thought the assignment would be good for my career."

They rode for a few miles before Colby asked, "When you learned Jacob's house had burned and his body was supposedly found inside, did you believe the news or did you suspect he was still alive right from the start?"

"I wanted to believe he had died. Elizabeth had invited me to stay with her. Sheriff McDougal came to her house to question me. He seemed sympathetic and knew I was struggling."

"Did you tell him your suspicions that Jacob was still alive?"

"Not at first, because I wanted to believe he was dead."

"Sounds as if something changed your mind."

She nodded. "I went for a run a few days later. Of course, I was still in shock, still grieving."

Colby reached for her hand. His touch offered support and a connection that had grown stronger in the last couple days. He was more than a partner. Much more.

"Jacob followed me." She shook her head. "I should re-phrase that—*someone* followed me. I headed along one of the trails that led into the country. There's a small pond. Mom's take their children there to feed the ducks and geese."

"But that day was different?"

Becca nodded. "Dark clouds had formed, and the wind picked up strength. I knew the rain would start soon, but I wanted to circle the pond before I returned to town."

She tugged at her hair with her free hand. "I heard some-one call my name."

"It was Jacob?"

"I never saw him, but I recognized his voice." Again her slender shoulders rose. "At least, I thought it was his voice. Rain fell in fat drops that stung my face and mixed with my tears. I ran as fast as I could, but the wind was against me, and the wet ground was slick. I—I kept looking over my shoulders."

"But you didn't see him?"

"No, but I sensed his presence. I told the sheriff. He told me to see a shrink and get some meds."

"Did you?"

"Of course not. I didn't need medication to know what I had heard. As soon as the bodies were interred, I drove back to Fort Campbell and put in for the CID. I needed to have the knowledge and strength and wherewithal to protect myself."

Colby squeezed her hand. "We'll find him, Becca."

She smiled ever so slightly. Much as she wanted Colby's help, she knew this fight was her own and too many had died already. She didn't want to pull him down with her. How could she endure if something happened to Colby because of her?

In the end, she'd have to confront Jacob. She had started the terrible spiral of events that had led to her sister and father being murdered and now even Elizabeth had been a victim of Jacob's crazed wrath.

Jacob was her problem. She'd started it, and she planned to finish it. She'd find Jacob and bring him to justice if it was the last thing she ever did.

Although relieved that Becca had shared some of what had happened long ago, Colby's heart tightened hearing the pain in her voice as she talked about Katie.

Thinking of his own sisters made her regret even more significant. The creep who had jilted his oldest sister, Gloria, was on his list of most heinous individuals.

His sister's broken heart had been hard enough to bear. He didn't want to think about any physical harm befalling her.

Plus, Becca had lost her father. Not that they seemed to have had the best relationship, but he was still her parent, and she had a strong sense of duty to family. Becca had wanted, and needed, her dad's attention and affection. He'd ignored her on that level and instead had made her feel less than important.

Colby thought of the future, wishing his tomorrows

would include Becca. Maybe some kids. He'd make sure they knew how much they were wanted and loved. Of course, he'd also ensure they were well mannered and respected authority, but every child needed love and affirmation.

He glanced at Becca. Her head rested against the back of the seat. He wasn't sure if she was sleeping, but he wouldn't do anything to wake her if she were.

Growing up must have been tough, always feeling she didn't measure up. Becca was a beautiful person inside and out, and Colby wanted to tell her how special she was and how important she was to him. She filled his thoughts and made their time together bright. He wanted to tell her a lot of things, which would have to wait until after the investigation.

Right now, he had to help her go back to her past. She carried a lot of pain that needed to be healed.

He knew the internal struggle guilt could cause. If only he hadn't transferred to another forward operating base, Ellen might still be alive. He'd left base earlier that same day. No one expected the mortar attack. He learned later that Ellen had been preoccupied with a report she needed to finish and had hesitated seeking shelter. He'd always been there before to push her to the safety of the bunker in time. Her delay had proved deadly when the second mortar hit.

Ellen had severed their relationship and probably would have ignored his help even if he hadn't left base, yet he still felt responsible for her death. The fact that he hadn't been there to protect her was a wound he wondered if he'd ever be able to heal. That's why protecting Becca was so important.

He glanced at her again. Becca's eyes were closed and her breath shallow. He and Becca both had holes in their hearts that needed to be filled. He wanted to help her. Maybe in helping her, he'd fix his own hurt. Or maybe he would never be able to forgive himself and redeem his past.

Either way, he wanted Becca to heal.

Please, Lord.

He pursed his lips. Did God listen to him anymore, or had He given up on Colby ever coming back to the fold?

Becca had mentioned having to carry a cross. She had her cross. Colby had his, as well.

If only he could help her.

If only he could help himself.

If only God would help both of them.

FIFTEEN

The house sat dark against the night sky. Becca had closed her eyes earlier and rested during the drive to Harmony, but she still felt the heavy weight of fatigue, probably brought on by the stress of returning home.

Seeing the house, the memories rushed upon her like the heat from the explosion on post. The unlatched door, the shadowed darkness of the room, her father's butchered body lying on the floor.

She climbed from the car, inhaling the cold, damp air and shivered. Colby placed his arm around her shoulders. She leaned into him, appreciating his warmth. He pulled her closer as if knowing the struggle raging inside her.

At this moment, she needed Colby more than she had ever needed anyone. He sensed that need and pulled her fully into his embrace.

A flicker of moonlight broke between the clouds and bathed them both in light. Colby hesitated and then slowly lowered his lips to hers. She clung to him like a lifeline, wanting to remain forever in his arms. The pain of her past eased momentarily, replaced with a hope for the future, something she had never allowed herself to consider since she had run away from Jacob.

Finding the inner courage to move forward, she pulled back ever so slightly. Colby's voice was husky with emotion when he spoke.

"We don't have to do this now," he told her. "We can come back another time."

She shook her head. "No. I won't run away again. Plus I want the body exhumed as soon as possible to prove it isn't Jacob."

"Without a chain of custody, I doubt whatever DNA sample you have will hold up in a court of law."

"Maybe not, but at least I'll know the truth."

"Whenever you're ready," Colby said, his support reassuring.

An owl hooted from the trees.

Becca squared her shoulders and nodded. "Let's go."

Arm in arm they climbed the steps to the porch, testing each one before placing their weight on the rotten boards. Two of the supporting braces were broken, causing the wooden planks to sag at an angle.

Colby remained at her side, encouraging her to go on. "Don't think about the past," he cautioned. "Stay in the present. Don't look back."

He switched on his Maglite and opened the door. Becca stepped inside, her gaze drawn to the spot where her father had died. A wide stain from his pooled blood still darkened the floorboards.

Colby rubbed his free hand over her arm. "Where do we go now?"

"Upstairs." She motioned him toward the narrow stairwell.

The old house creaked with each step.

Slowly and deliberately, she climbed to the second floor. Colby's footfalls followed behind her. The steady pull of air in and out of his lungs assured her of his presence.

I'm not alone. Colby's with me. This is now.

The dank and musty smell of the old house drew her back in time. For an instant, she was again the defiant youth. Too strong-willed, her father had often said.

How many nights had she retreated to her bedroom dreaming of what her life could be? In those days, she had believed in love and happiness and goodness. Perhaps it had been a way to escape the reality of her existence.

Her father's room sat on the left. She walked past without glancing through the doorway. What did she need to see?

Instead, she was drawn to the open door at the end of the hall. Hesitating for a moment at the threshold, she pulled in a deep breath and stepped into the tiny room, smaller than she had remembered. Her gaze flicked over the single bed and faded quilt. In the corner, mouse droppings were evidence of the tiny creatures that lived here now.

Using both her hands, she pushed the bed aside and shooed away the thick cobwebs as she dropped to her knees. "Shine the light on the floor."

Colby angled the Maglite over where she knelt. She ran the tips of her fingers across the floorboards, searching for the uneven plank.

Why couldn't she find it?

She pushed the bed farther from the wall and expanded her search until her hand snagged against a sharp sliver of wood. She pulled back.

Colby leaned closer. "What's wrong, honey?"

Becca shook her head. "A splinter, that's all."

Focused on the uneven plank, she dug at the wood. It failed to budge.

"Let me try." Colby handed her the flashlight and knelt beside her on the floor. He picked at the irregular edge and was finally able to pry the plank loose. Using two hands, he eased the board free.

Becca aimed the light into space under the flooring. *Empty!*

She moaned ever so quietly and turned to Colby as if he'd known what she had expected to find. "It's not here."

He took the flashlight from her hand and angled it farther into the hollowed-out area until something metallic reflected in the darkness.

Her treasure box.

Relief swept over her. She clawed at the small container

jammed in the back of the cubbyhole. Her fingers eased it forward until she could lift it free.

Her heart pounded in her chest, just as had often happened as a girl when she removed the tin box to look at her precious keepsakes.

Tonight was no different with the steady thump of her pulse and an overwhelming need to glance over her shoulder to ensure she was alone.

Only she wasn't alone tonight. Colby was kneeling next to her. His presence brought a sense of security and dispelled the darkness that surrounded her youth. She leaned into him, feeling his strength.

He rubbed his hand over her shoulder and waited patiently as she stared at the tin, not quite ready to expose the past.

The bond between them had grown even stronger this evening. She smiled, remembering his kiss and the concern and understanding that was so evident in his gaze.

Colby seemed to care about her in a special way just as she was beginning to realize the depth of her feelings for him. Tonight she was all too aware of his willingness to enter into the pain of her past, yet when she opened the box, he would know what she had always wanted to remain hidden.

She closed her eyes for a long moment before she removed the lid. Glancing down, she saw the bits and pieces of her childhood, so seemingly insignificant, yet each an important facet of her life.

A pretty rock that sparkled like gold. *Fool's gold,* her father called it, but special to a child who had nothing and wanted something of her own. A tiny fossil that opened her mind to the vastness of creation and what had been millenniums ago. A fake pearl necklace she found along the roadway. The clasp was broken and had, no doubt, dropped unnoticed from some woman's neck. Becca had often draped the pearls around her own, knowing her father would call it an abomination if he ever saw her wearing jewelry.

"Your necklace?" Colby asked.

"Something I found and shouldn't have kept."

"What about the fossil and speckled rock?"

"They reminded me of the beauty of God's creation." She smiled ruefully. "I was a romantic as a youth."

He touched her cheek, and she turned to face him. "But no longer?"

Regret tugged at her heart. "I learned too quickly about the reality of life."

He nodded slowly. "Seeing the darkness of the world at too young an age can be painful."

She rested her head on his shoulder, grateful for his presence, before she removed the other items from the box and lay them aside. An envelope sat at the bottom, brittle as parchment and almost as yellow.

Colby angled the light. "Is this what you came to find?"

She nodded. Years ago, she had used a knife to open the envelope, leaving the sealed flap intact. Slowly, she withdrew the note written in script with broad strokes by a black pen.

Meet me tonight at the covered bridge.
Yours affectionately, Jacob Yoder

How could she have been so gullible, so naive, so unaware of how a man could break a young girl's heart? Jacob had never showed up that night, nor the next or the one following. Instead he had turned his charms on the widow Mary.

Becca hadn't seen him again until she was forced to care for the woman Jacob, by that time, had married. Thrown together again, he had hoped to take up where they had left off. At least, Becca had learned from her earlier mistake.

Jacob, on the other hand, didn't understand why Becca shunned his advances. How could he think she would succumb to his desires when he'd rejected her to marry another?

She still couldn't forgive her youthful infatuation with the handsome stranger who had whispered words that filled her mind with the possibilities of a life together. Her innocent flirting and inability to see the consequences of her actions had led to so much pain, so many deaths. She had to stop Jacob so what she had started long ago could finally end.

Colby called Lewis Stone on the way back to town. "Special Agent Becca Miller and I are heading to your office. We have Jacob Yoder's DNA on an envelope he licked some years ago."

"I'll meet you there," the sheriff said.

Going home had weighed Becca down. Colby saw it in the hesitation in her step and the slump of her shoulders. Surely the memories of the night she had found her father and sister must be affecting her in addition to knowing that Jacob could be nearby.

She had been barely eighteen. How easy for an older man to tease a young, impressionable woman reared in the closed environment of an Amish community.

Jacob hadn't thought of Becca's feelings. More than likely he wanted to control every situation, never weighing how his actions could impact the young woman.

Lights from town appeared in the distance. Colby drove toward the main square and passed the turnoff to Elizabeth's house. Becca glanced out the window at the side street of modest homes.

Her heart must be breaking as she thought of the woman who had assisted her in escaping Jacob's control. A woman who was eventually killed by the very man she had helped Becca elude.

Colby turned left at the square. The sheriff's office sat

on the corner. He pulled into the parking area and rounded the car to help Becca with the door.

"Do you want to stay in the car and let me handle this?"

She shook her head. "It's my story to tell, Colby, but thank you for trying to protect me."

With the evidence bag in hand, they stepped into the glare of overhead fluorescent lights. Lewis met them in the hallway. They shook hands, and he ushered them into his office and invited them to sit.

"Tell me what you've got," he said, settling into the swivel chair behind his desk.

Becca placed the paper bag in front of the sheriff. "A sealed note Jacob Yoder gave me approximately ten years ago. Forensics will be able to uncover his DNA from the saliva on the flap of the envelope."

"There's no chain of custody," Lewis pointed out.

"I'm aware the evidence won't be admissible in court."

She moved forward in the chair and glanced at Colby, as if for support. "I..." She shook her head. "We want the body that was found in the Yoder farmhouse exhumed and DNA testing done. My suspicion is that it wasn't Jacob Yoder, but rather his brother, Ezekiel."

"Did Jacob kill his brother?" the sheriff asked.

"At this point, I don't know, but I'd also like his wife Mary's body exhumed and testing to be done for any trace of a poisonous substance."

"He killed her?"

Becca nodded. "I think he was slowly poisoning his wife, which led to her declining health."

Colby filled the chief in on the similar case in Tennessee. "We can't be sure, but the man fit Jacob's description, including a scar on his left cheek, and there seems to be a pattern."

Lewis stared at both of them for a long moment. Colby

couldn't determine which direction the sheriff was leaning toward.

Finally he grabbed a pencil and sheet of paper from his desk drawer. "Give me the name of the police department you talked to up north. I'll contact them and include that information in my request for both bodies to be exhumed."

Lewis copied the information Colby provided and then said, "You realize the DNA testing will take time."

Becca nodded. "But you'll start the process, which is what I want."

"I can't guarantee that I'll get the go-ahead on this, but there seem to be enough unanswered questions to warrant an exhumation."

"Thank you." Both agents stood.

"Becca, watch your back," Lewis cautioned. "If what you've told me is true, Jacob will stop at nothing to complete the job he started long ago."

Colby knew the chief was right, but hearing the danger expressed aloud cast a pall on both of them as they drove back to Fort Rickman.

Had Jacob killed Becca's father and sister to get at her? If so, just as Lewis had mentioned, Jacob would stop at nothing to finish the job he had started years earlier.

SIXTEEN

After a fitful night's sleep, Becca woke to reveille as the bugle call sounded over a loudspeaker on the nearby parade field. She quickly dressed for the new day and arrived at work just as a company of soldiers passed in formation. The singsong rhythm of their Jody calls floated through the crisp morning air.

Entering CID headquarters, she returned Sergeant Raynard Otis's salute. His welcoming smile provided a positive lift from the darkness of last night.

"Do you ever go home, Ray?" she asked.

"Yes, ma'am. But I like to beat the boss to work and you know Chief Wilson is an early bird."

"Is he in his office now?"

"Roger that, ma'am." Ray checked his watch. "The chief arrived fifteen minutes ago, which was ten minutes after I logged on to my computer."

"Anyone with him?"

"Not that I know of. You want me to let him know you're headed his way?"

"Thanks, but I need to pull some information together first."

Ray pointed over his shoulder. "Coffee's hot, ma'am. I brought doughnuts. Help yourself."

"I'll forego the sugar, but coffee is just what I need. Thanks, Ray."

After pouring a cup, she logged in to her computer and pulled up the list of Amish communities she had compiled. There were a few more towns in Kentucky she wanted to contact before she started looking at Ohio and Pennsylvania. Those states were heavily populated with Amish and would take longer to process.

The first two calls she made provided no information. The third police department said they were tied up with change of shift and would call her back after 8:00 a.m.

Disconnecting, she smiled, hearing Colby greet Sergeant Otis. She met Colby at the coffeepot and held out her cup for a refill.

"Kind of late getting to work this morning, aren't you, Voss?" she teased.

He laughed as he filled her mug. "A little friendly office competition, eh, Miller?"

"Just thinking about the early bird and the worm."

"I'm definitely the worm this morning."

She raised her brow. "Rough night?"

"Just wondering when we'll make progress with this investigation."

She stirred creamer into her coffee and then took a sip. "I'm calling a few more police departments in Kentucky. Then I'd like to talk to the chief."

"Remember what he told you, Becca?"

"How could I forget? Stay in the office and let you do the legwork."

Colby nodded. "That's it. I should talk to him."

"I want to be there."

"Just let me take the lead. We need to know if that disgruntled contractor from Macon has turned into someone of interest."

"Shall we mention that the Yoder gravesite may be exhumed?"

Colby returned the coffee carafe to the stand. "Let's wait until we have the go-ahead from Harmony."

"That works for me. I'll let you know if the phone calls pay off this morning."

Two hours later, Colby poked his head into her cubicle. "Anything yet?"

"I'm waiting for a return call."

Before he could reply, her phone rang.

She raised the receiver. "Criminal Investigation Division, Fort Rickman, Georgia, Special Agent Miller."

"This is Wanda at Post Transportation."

Becca pushed the phone closer to her ear. "Has my shipment from Germany arrived on post?"

"We tried to contact you yesterday at your BOQ."

"Didn't you hear about the explosion? My BOQ was destroyed. You should have called my cell."

Colby rolled his eyes. Transportation Departments were known for their less-than-stellar customer service.

"Your landline is the only number listed on the paperwork," Wanda said over the phone. "I tracked you down through the post locator."

Becca remembered specifically providing both her land and mobile numbers, but she didn't want to argue with a clerk who was just trying to do her job. "Do you have information about my shipment, Wanda?"

"It's scheduled to be delivered this afternoon."

"Today?"

"Yes, ma'am. At two o'clock. I've got your address as Eisenhower Avenue."

"That's my old BOQ. The one that was destroyed."

"Sorry to hear that, ma'am. Where shall we deliver your shipment?"

"Ah…" She looked at Colby for help. "I need to check with the housing department. Someone in your office told me it would be two more weeks before my things arrived."

"Yes, ma'am. But if we don't have a point of delivery, we'll be forced to unload the truck at the warehouse and reschedule delivery at a later time. We're currently back-logged seven days."

"Give me through the lunch hour to come up with something. Again, I'm sorry for any confusion this may have caused."

Becca hung up and grabbed her purse. "I need a BOQ. Can you talk to Wilson alone?"

"Roger that. Let me know where you end up." He grabbed her arm. "By the way, there's an empty set of quarters on my street."

"That sounds like a solution to my housing problems." She squeezed his hand. "Thanks, Colby."

She hurried to the post housing office and waited far too long for a clerk to process the three people ahead of her.

By the time her name was called, it was almost one o'clock. She quickly explained the situation and decided to accept the quarters near Colby, sight unseen. After filling out the necessary forms, she grabbed the keys and called transportation on the way out the door. She gave them the delivery address, relieved that she would arrive at her new home just minutes ahead of the moving van.

The two-bedroom apartment was clean and in fairly good shape. She could see Colby's place from her backyard, which made her outlook even brighter. Being stationed at Fort Rickman would be a positive experience after all.

Colby gave her the space she needed and didn't ask too many questions. He hadn't demanded details about the note from Jacob Yoder, which she appreciated, yet they were dealing with a murder investigation. Eventually he would need to know all the information surrounding the case. Information she didn't want to reveal.

She'd ignored logic years ago and reacted with her heart, which had cost her dearly and claimed the lives of her father and sister. As much as she wanted to be open with Colby, she had to be careful. She couldn't make another deadly mistake.

Colby made a quick stop after work and then headed to his BOQ eager to see Becca and find out whether her shipment had arrived. He'd called her cell a number of times, but she hadn't answered, and the phone had gone to voice mail.

If the shipment had arrived, she was probably busy unpacking. The process could take days. Knowing Becca, she would push hard to get settled as soon as possible.

The moving van was just leaving when Colby pulled into the parking lot. He headed to the previously empty apartment and smiled when Becca opened the door.

"Welcome to the neighborhood." He held up a paper bag. "I stopped for food on the way home. Teriyaki chicken and lo mein. I thought you might want to take a break for dinner. I can help you unpack if you'd prefer to eat later."

She inhaled the rich aroma and sighed with pleasure. "Chinese sounds great. I missed lunch, and I'm starving. You must have read my mind."

"Any damage to your things?"

"The usual nicks and scratches, but nothing that can't be repaired."

She motioned him inside and gave him a quick hug in greeting before she pointed to the living room. "The coffee table is the only uncluttered space."

"The Wok provided paper plates and plastic utensils. I told them to pack extra napkins."

She laughed. "You were thinking like a true soldier. I've got colas and water in the fridge. Or I could brew coffee. That is, if I can find the coffeemaker."

"Let's keep it simple with a cola. Can I get them?"

"Sure. Pull two from the fridge while I spray some cleaner over the glass top on the table."

He returned with two colas and sat on the floor across from her at the low coffee table.

"Why don't you say the blessing?" she suggested.

He bowed his head, feeling a bit out of touch. Hopefully his sister's insistence that the Lord was a God of forgiveness was legit.

"Dear God," he prayed. "We thank You for the arrival of Becca's shipment. Help her bring order to the chaos and allow this BOQ to be a good home during her assignment to Fort Rickman. Help both of us with this investigation, and thank You for those who prepared the food we are about to eat. May it nourish our bodies, and may You find us open to Your promptings as we face the rest of the day together."

"Amen," they said in unison, and then both laughed.

"I'm not used to extemporaneous prayer," he confessed.

"Really? You fooled me. If I prayed, I'd be afraid of a lightning strike."

He dug in the bag and pulled out two containers. "There's white rice and condiments. Also egg rolls."

She placed one of the egg rolls on her plate and then reached for the rice and spooned out a large portion. "I'll take a little of each dish, if that's okay with you." She arranged both over rice, and he followed suit.

Colby hadn't realized how hungry he'd been.

Before he finished, his phone chirped. "Which reminds me," he said as he pulled it from his pocket, "I tried to call you today."

"Yikes. I left my cell in my purse." She got up and headed into her bedroom and returned seconds later with her phone in hand. "Sorry. I turned down the volume on the ring."

He smiled as he glanced at his sister's name on his own phone screen and raised the cell to his ear. "Hey, Gloria. What's up?"

"Just wondering how my brother's doing."

"Eating Chinese and welcoming a new neighbor to post. Can I call you back?"

"Sure, but I hear something in your voice that hasn't been there since you redeployed home. What's her name?"

"You're jumping to conclusions."

"Don't keep secrets, Colby."

"Are Mom and Dad okay?"

"Busy and content. So are the rest of the clan. We miss you, Colby. You need to come home for a visit."

"I'd like that. Now what about you?"

"I'm okay."

"Anyone new in your life?"

"I'll be the first to let you know."

"It's time, Gloria."

"That's what I told you, my dear brother, four months ago. At least you sound happy."

He looked across the table at Becca and smiled. "I am happy. Talk to you soon."

"You and your sister must be close," Becca said when he disconnected.

"We are, but she insists on checking up on me. She's older, by fourteen months, and thinks that gives her control over her baby brother."

"You're lucky to have her."

"I know that. Plus, I've got four more that are just like her although not quite as interested in my well-being. Probably because they're younger and focused on their own lives."

"I'm jealous," she joked, but he knew there was an element of truth to her statement.

"I can loan you Gloria."

"She's the one who was stood up at the altar?"

He nodded. "She says she's okay, but I know better."

"Maybe she needs more time to work through the rejection."

Colby took a swig of his cola and then hesitated, wondering if he should ask the question that continued to circle through his mind. "We didn't talk about the note last night, Becca. Was there something between you and Jacob?"

Her cheeks flushed, and she dropped her gaze. "I don't want to discuss it, Colby."

"It might help if you could—"

"—talk about it?" She bristled. "There's nothing to talk about. Besides, I'm not your sister."

"I wasn't implying you were. It's just I could tell how upset you were last night."

"I was upset going back into the house where my father and sister were murdered."

"I know." He patted his chest. "Remember, I'm on your side. We're in this together, Becca."

She shook her head. "That's not true. We're investigating together because that's the way Wilson wants it, but you don't have anything to do with Jacob's murders. You weren't the one responsible for what he did."

"Why do you feel responsible?"

She shook her head as if realizing she'd said too much. "I don't."

"It's because of Katie, isn't it?"

He saw the hurt in her eyes and knew he'd found the sweet spot of her pain.

"You're not at fault, Becca."

"You don't know what happened, Colby."

"Then tell me."

"It doesn't have any bearing on the investigation. Besides, some things are personal and don't need to be shared. Can you live with that?"

He nodded. "I'll have to. You pretend to be hard as steel, but there's always a part you keep hidden. That's the part I want to know more about."

"It's the part I'll never share, Colby."

"You were so young. Jacob Yoder was a man who thought

only of himself. Whatever happened, you weren't to blame. He's the one who forced his way into your life and then later into your home."

She glanced at her watch. "I'm too tired to discuss this any further. Why don't you take your Chinese food and go home?"

"Becca, please."

"Please, what? Please, tell me more about how you fell in love with a madman?" She shook her head and stood. "I'll see you at the office in the morning, but right now, I want to be alone."

"We don't have to talk about Jacob."

"We don't have to talk about anything." She pointed to the door. "Do I need to see you out?"

He threw down his napkin and huffed. "I know the way."

Colby left, frustrated more with himself than with Becca, and headed back to his own apartment. He shouldn't have pressed her for information, but they had an investigation to solve, and Becca might have some of the answers. Why wouldn't she let him into her secret past?

SEVENTEEN

Becca shoved the rest of the Chinese food in the fridge. The rather heated discussion she'd had with Colby had dampened her enthusiasm for food. Nor did she feel like unpacking another box, but she had a houseful of items that needed to be arranged, and if she didn't do the work, no one would.

Certainly not Colby. She couldn't rely on him to help. He would broach questions that upset her and would force her to raise her voice and ask him to leave again.

What was wrong with her? She should have tried to change the subject. Instead, she had gotten hot under the collar, as the guys at work often said.

She ran water in the sink and began to wash the dishes she had unpacked earlier. Once they were put away, she glanced out the back door window, noting the dark skyline. Night had come too early. Either that or the afternoon had passed too quickly.

The uncovered window made her feel vulnerable, which she didn't like. She'd hang curtains tomorrow or call post maintenance about installing blinds.

Jacob Yoder was still alive and out there some place, although she doubted he would try to come on post since the military police had enhanced security. She should feel secure, but after the tiff with Colby, all she felt was confusion.

Glancing at her phone, she considered calling him and apologizing for her sharp words. Whenever she was afraid, she tended to lash out too quickly, just as she had done this evening. The look on Colby's face told her he hadn't expected her affront.

Nor did he deserve her wrath. Not Colby with his compassionate eyes and strong arms, which made her feel special in their embrace.

Convinced she needed to apologize, Becca grabbed her purse, flicked off the lights and hurried to the front door. Before she turned the knob, a sound caused her to look through the house to the backyard. Something or someone moved in the shadows outside.

She stepped into the living area and peeked from the window. Her new place sat at the far end of the row of townhouse apartments, and a thick wooded area surrounded her on two sides. The leaves in the trees swayed in the wind. Surely that was what had drawn her attention.

The tension in her chest eased. She rolled her shoulders, relaxing her muscles. Letting out a deep breath, she started to turn away from the window.

Then something caught her eye. Something or someone.

She backed into the corner and narrowed her gaze.

Tension pounded up her spine. The muscles in her back tightened again. Blood rushed to her head.

A man stood at the edge of the undergrowth. Tall, perhaps Jacob's height, dressed in black.

She glanced at the overstuffed chair sitting near the window and thought of a box she had unpacked earlier. She hurried to her bedroom. Digging through a pile of clothing, she found the costume she had worn for the German-American Club's on-post carnival celebration. Along with the outfit was a curly wig, the color of her own hair. She grabbed a bathrobe and pillows off the bed.

Returning to the hall, she dropped to the floor and duck crawled across the living area, holding the items she had collected in her arms.

With swift, sure movements, she wrapped the robe around the pillows and arranged them in the chair. She placed the wig on a smaller throw pillow that she positioned on top of the large, bed pillows. If someone looked in the window, they'd see the back of the chair and hopefully mistake the wig and arrangement of pillows for a person. Namely her.

Crawling out of the room, she turned on the small lamp in the entryway. Diffuse light angled toward the living area. The stuffed dummy was visible but not distinguishable to someone peering through the window.

She opened her purse and drew out her gun and cell phone and keys. No matter who was outside, she needed backup. More than that, she needed Colby.

Becca pushed the preset button for his cell. Before it rang, she opened the front door and stepped onto the sidewalk.

The call went to voice mail. Why wouldn't he answer? Was he angry because of her earlier outburst? She'd try again when she had a clearer view of the backyard Peeping Tom.

She rounded the BOQ and slowly inched her way through the undergrowth, taking care not to make a sound. The snap of a twig or the crunch of dried leaves could cause him to flee.

Thirty feet from the perp, she halted.

Tree frogs and cicadas filled the night. A cool breeze blew through her clothing.

Ever so slowly, the man in black approached the lighted window.

She held her breath. Just a few more feet and she'd be able to see his face.

A door closed.

The man startled at the sound.

A cold chill wrapped around Becca's heart.

Colby hurried down his back steps, carrying something in his hand, and walked across the common rear area heading for her BOQ.

The man moved away from the window.

"Stop." She stepped from the shadows, her gun raised. "CID."

He flicked a glance over his shoulder and ran into the darkness.

Becca raced after him.

The prowler ducked into the thick, wooded area. She followed. Brambles caught at her legs, and twigs slapped her face, but she kept pushing forward.

Behind her came the sound of footfalls and the pull of air, just as she had heard in her dreams. Only this time Jacob wasn't chasing her, it was Colby.

She dashed on to where the trees parted. To one side was a drop off to a creek bed that led to the river. On the other was a series of military buildings, each providing shadowed areas where the assailant could hide.

Colby caught up with her. "Where'd he go?"

She shook her head. "I lost him."

"Did he hurt you?" Colby reached for her arm.

She shrugged away from him, angry that her attempt to identify the guy had failed. "You scared him away, Colby. He was walking into the light. I needed to see his face. Two more seconds and I would have known if it was Jacob."

"What were you doing outside?"

"I set up a decoy and then circled around the house to wait him out," she explained.

"You didn't call me."

"I tried." She held up her phone as if to confirm the call.

Colby's face twisted with frustration. "My phone never rang."

Had she made a mistake and called the wrong number? She shook her head, unwilling to back down. "Once I was outside, I didn't want to make any noise that might startle him so I couldn't call you again."

"You could have gotten killed."

"I had the upper hand, Colby. Until—"

"Until I walked outside? What if one of the other neighbors had emptied their trash or had gone for an evening stroll? If the perp had a weapon, the neighbors could have been caught in the cross fire. Did you think about that?"

She hadn't. She'd only been thinking of identifying the perp. Squaring her shoulders, she turned to retrace her steps. Behind her, she heard Colby call in a report to CID Headquarters.

"Notify the military police. Close off post. Check every car that leaves Fort Rickman. Cordon off the area around Sheridan Road. Set up roadblocks and have the military police patrol the area on foot. We need to find this guy."

He hesitated for a moment.

"Yes, notify Chief Wilson and General Cameron."

With a huff, Becca shoved a branch aside and walked through the woods back to her BOQ. Colby was right. She shouldn't have tackled the problem alone, but she had tried to call him, even if he didn't believe her.

Sirens sounded, and a swarm of military police spilled from their patrol cars and quickly fanned out to search the area.

She knew the main gate was locked down and each car leaving post was being searched, all because she hadn't been able to stop Jacob.

Using large battery-operated spotlights, the crime-scene team searched the wooded area where the prowler had been hunkered down.

"The perp didn't leave much to go on," one of the men told Becca.

A soldier approached her, holding something in his hand. "These were on the grass, ma'am. Special Agent Voss said they belong to you."

She took the bouquet of flowers, yellow roses, each flower a perfect bud almost ready to open. The flowers Colby had probably purchased at the Shopette on post and planned to give her as he walked toward her BOQ. Had they been a way to make right their earlier disagreement? Now there was no hope of rectifying the situation.

A lump filled Becca's throat. She was tired and cold and upset that she hadn't handled the situation correctly. Once again, she'd tried to do everything herself instead of calling in backup.

With a heavy heart, she walked into her apartment. The military police and crime-scene techs could continue to work outside, but she wanted to put the flowers in water and then sit by herself in the dark.

She never should have come to Fort Rickman. She had allowed her attraction for Colby to get in the way of the investigation, and that could prove deadly.

EIGHTEEN

Colby arrived at work early the next morning, hoping to talk to Becca before he briefed Wilson on what had happened. She wasn't in her cubicle, and Wilson saw him in the hallway and motioned Colby into his office.

"Tell me about last night," Wilson said as he slipped into the chair behind his desk.

"Agent Miller noticed someone outside her BOQ, sir. She rigged a dummy in a chair in her living room, left her apartment through the front door and circled around trying to spot the perp when he approached her window."

"Seems her plan backfired."

"I'm probably to blame for that, sir. He saw me exit my BOQ and fled. Agent Miller followed in pursuit. I did, as well. We lost him in the training area."

"Did Agent Miller call you for help?"

"Yes, sir, she did. Unfortunately, I didn't hear my phone."

"What about the military police?"

"I don't believe she contacted them."

"So she attempted to capture the assailant without calling for backup?" Wilson's tone was stern.

"In all fairness, sir, Agent Miller was hoping to get a positive ID on the prowler. The Harmony, Alabama, sheriff still hasn't gotten a court order to exhume the body in Jacob Yoder's grave. Becca needs proof he's alive, which is only complicated by the Amish avoidance of photos. As you know, we don't have a snapshot of the guy."

"Do you think Yoder is alive?"

"I'm not sure, sir, but someone is out to do her harm."

"I told Becca to remain at her desk. That means she shouldn't be staging booby traps in her backyard."

"Yes, sir. But she probably didn't want the opportunity to pass her by."

"Hauling an Amish man in for murder before the first farmers' market and craft fair on Fort Rickman could put a damper on the festivities."

"I understand your concern, sir."

"Which has no bearing on us bringing him in, no matter what activity the commanding general's wife has planned."

"Yes, sir."

"I'll call the Harmony sheriff and see if I can't encourage them to exhume the body. You mentioned having a DNA specimen that can be traced to Yoder?"

"Yes, sir. An envelope he sealed."

"Someone was lucky. Any idea how they uncovered the envelope?"

"Ah...." Colby wanted to tell Wilson the truth, but he also wanted to protect Becca. "I believe it was retrieved in one of the old Amish homes."

"Someone was saying their prayers."

"I'm sure they were, sir."

Wilson pursed his lips and lowered his gaze, signaling the meeting was over.

"Thank you, sir." Before Colby could do an about-face, a tap sounded at the door.

The chief glanced up. "Enter."

Becca stepped into the office. Her eyes widened when she saw Colby.

"I was just leaving," he assured her.

"Hold up, Colby," Wilson said. "You and Becca have been working together. You need to stay."

"Uh, sir, I've got some calls to make."

"This shouldn't take long," Wilson insisted.

Inwardly, Colby groaned. Last night, his relationship with Becca had hit rock bottom. Being present when she faced the boss would only do more harm.

Becca didn't want to believe him or trust him. She had her own ideas about how an investigation should be run, and Colby wasn't the top man on her go-to list. As far as he knew, she probably wanted to team up with one of the other agents.

Becca was a problem.

Not to the investigation but to his heart.

Finding Colby in the chief's office made Becca's day go from bad to worse, and it was only 7:00 a.m.

"Ray said you wanted to see me, sir."

"A lot happened last night."

"A prowler, sir, outside my BOQ."

"You think it's the same man who caused the explosion?"

She glanced at Colby who stood to the side, hands clasped behind his back in a typical army, parade-rest stance with his eyes lowered.

"That might be putting too many pieces together and getting the wrong picture, sir. I didn't get close enough to ID the Peeping Tom."

"But it could have been Jacob Yoder?"

"That's a possibility."

"What did I tell you about this case, Becca?"

She swallowed. "That I should handle things from my desk and let Special Agent Voss do the legwork"

Wilson nodded. "Did you comply with my request?"

"As best I could, sir."

"Did that include setting a decoy to catch the man last night?"

Evidently Colby had been very forthright with the chief. "I merely wanted to distract him. The danger to me was minimal."

Colby cleared his throat.

Even more anxiety bubbled up within her.

Wilson steepled his fingers. "I hardly think going outside to surprise an assailant is a protective measure. In my mind, you were putting yourself in danger."

"I planned to call law enforcement."

"But did you?" His brow arched.

She hesitated. "I tried to contact Agent Voss. The call went to voice mail."

"Did you leave a message?"

"I—I, uh, ran out of time."

Again the raised brow. "What does that mean?"

"It means I needed to move closer to the prowler while his attention was focused on my back door."

"Actually, his focus was trained on the dummy inside that he thought was you."

Another detail Colby had shared with Wilson. "Yes, sir."

"You drew your weapon?"

"When he started to flee."

"Yet you weren't in danger?"

Heat warmed her neck. "I had hoped to apprehend him before any exchange of gunfire."

"Therefore the situation you walked into could have been life threatening."

"In hindsight, that might be the case."

Wilson cleared his throat and adjusted himself in his chair as he seemingly mulled over his next comment. "You were fortunate this time, Becca. But I don't like agents who strike out on their own. Everyone in this organization needs to follow the rules and my directions. Is that understood?"

"Yes, sir."

"I want you to work on the security plans for the farmers' market and craft fair. Nothing else. Is that understood?"

"Yes, sir."

"Under no circumstances are you to knowingly put yourself or anyone else in danger."

"Sir, I didn't think—"

Wilson held up his hand to cut her off. "That's it exactly, Becca. You didn't think."

He handed her a piece of paper containing a phone number. "Call the general's wife. Mrs. Cameron had a request to make concerning the market."

She took the paper and nodded. "Thank you, sir."

Unwilling to even glance in Colby's direction, she hurried from the office and let out a lungful of air she had been holding too long. Her cheeks burned as she recalled the scoldings her father had given her of old. Today, she felt like a wayward child who had done something wrong. Colby's presence only compounded her humiliation.

She should have contacted law enforcement immediately after seeing the man in her backyard. Of course, she'd thought she could take care of it herself.

Why did she always have to be so headstrong and self-sufficient? Maybe because no one had ever been there for her in the past.

She hurried along the hallway to her cubicle, dropped the message from Mrs. Cameron on her desk and grabbed her purse. Tension pounded through her head, and she blinked back tears. The last thing she wanted to do was cry or let anyone in the office see her agitation. Especially not Colby.

She raced out the back door and ran to her car, not sure where she was headed until she turned onto Eisenhower Drive. Pulling to a stop, she stared at the burned wreckage of her BOQ.

Looking back, she wished she had handled things differently. But what was done, was done.

Sitting in her parked car with no one around, she started to cry, feeling the entire struggle from the last week well up within her. She'd tried to keep her secrets buried, but Colby had pushed his way into her life, and now he knew too much about the mistakes she had made.

All she'd ever wanted in life was to be loved, but it always eluded her. Maybe she didn't know how to accept love, and if she couldn't accept love how could she return it to someone else? Today, she realized "that someone else" had a name.

Colby.

Colby sat in his cubicle, wondering when Becca would return to CID Headquarters. She'd been away from her desk a long time, and that worried him. He wanted her to know they were in this together.

In hindsight, Colby should have run after her when she left Wilson's office. Instead, he had tried to ease Wilson's frustration by mentioning his own regret at walking head-long into a situation Becca seemed to have had under control. Whether Wilson bought into what Colby shared was debatable, and by the time he left the chief, Becca was nowhere to be found.

Surely she wouldn't be gone long.

To kill time, he pulled the list of Amish communities from the folder on his desk and did a computer search, working his way into Ohio.

None of the police departments he called had information about any violent crimes in their local areas. He was relieved as well as discouraged. Everything was still so nebulous when it came to Jacob Yoder. They weren't even sure he was alive.

Going back and forth between search engines, he tried various key words and finally pulled up information about a small Amish community just across the Ohio River from Kentucky. He called the closest police department in Ohio, found nothing of interest and, on a whim, contacted law enforcement on the Kentucky side. Although Colby doubted the call would be productive, the name of the town was Harmony, and the coincidence of two towns with the same name wasn't lost on him.

He tapped in the digits for the local sheriff.

"Harmony Sheriff's Office. This is Deputy Oaks."

Colby quickly introduced himself and asked about any nearby Amish communities.

"Not on this side of the Ohio. Cross over the bridge and you'll find a number of Amish farms."

"I'm looking for an Amish drifter who preys on lonely widows. He helps with handy work and farm chores and often ends up moving in with them."

"What's the bottom line?"

"A string of older women who become ill or infirmed and die within a year or two of meeting him."

"Nice guy, eh?"

"You got that right." Colby pushed back in his chair, ready to disconnect. "Just wanted to check. Thanks for your time."

"What about non-Amish?" the deputy asked.

"Pardon?"

"We had a widow by the name of Lucy Reynolds who took up with a drifter. She needed help. He was a willing worker. Six months later, she ends up dead."

Colby straightened in his chair. "I'm listening."

"The widow told a friend he'd asked her to marry him but she refused. Still she kept him on as a hired hand. He stayed in a room in the back of the garage until he eventually left town."

"What happened to Mrs. Reynolds?"

"She died two weeks later. Fell down an old well on her property. A friend of hers said she'd taken money out of her savings account a few days earlier. The cash was never found. Plus, her car was gone."

"What make and model?"

"A 2005 Crown Vic, metallic blue in color."

The car they'd seen in the barn. "Are you sure the guy wasn't Amish?"

"He wasn't dressed like the Amish and he drove a car, although he did have a beard."

"Do you have a description?"

"I can do better than that. I've got a picture. That friend of the widow's was an amateur photographer. She snapped a photograph of Lucy and captured the drifter in the background of the shot. I can fax a copy to you. It's attached to a rundown of the widow's estate, which I'll include, as well."

"Perfect. Thanks." Colby relayed the CID fax number.

"I've got a city council meeting that will tie me up for the next few hours," Deputy Oaks continued. "I'll try to send the fax before I leave the office. Otherwise, it'll get to you by the end of the day."

Colby disconnected, feeling that the tide was changing. Hopefully, the photo would confirm the drifter was Jacob Yoder.

His phone rang and he heard the Alabama sheriff's voice on the other end of the line. "Hey, Lewis, what can I do for you?"

"Just wanted you to know we're expecting to get the go-ahead for exhuming Jacob Yoder's body. Also his wife's. The DNA from the envelope is being tested. Two exhumed bodies might speed the process and ensure everyone knows this case has priority."

Colby appreciated the chief's interest in getting to the bottom of the investigation.

"I thought you might want to be here when we open the graves," Lewis added.

"Looks like the investigation is taking a turn in the right direction. I may have a photograph of Jacob Yoder, although it won't get to my desk until later today. I'd like you to see the picture and then distribute it to your folks so they can be on the lookout for him. I'll have someone from here scan it and send it to me."

Colby looked at his watch. He was still worried about

Becca, but he had to get to Harmony as soon as possible. "I'll meet you at the gravesite in two hours."

"Sounds good. The Amish cemetery sits back from the main road, on the right, not far from Hershberger's farm and Yoder's old property. You should be able to spot us from the road."

Despite Becca's hasty departure, Colby wanted her to know about the exhumation. He peered into her cubicle, surprised she hadn't returned.

He found Ray Otis at his desk. "Any idea where Special Agent Miller went?"

"I'm not sure, sir. Maybe Quarters One. Mrs. Cameron called earlier and left a message. She wanted Becca to pick up some papers concerning the farmers' market."

"Do you know when she plans to be back in the office?"

"Negative, sir."

"I'm expecting a fax, Ray, sometime in the next few hours. It's from a sheriff's office in Kentucky. When it arrives, scan a copy and send it to my email."

"Will do, sir."

Colby hurried outside. Becca had pushed for the disinterment and would, no doubt, be relieved to know it was in the works. Maybe the news would help soften the struggle between them.

On the way to his car, he tried her cell, but she didn't answer. No reason to leave a voice mail. If she wanted to talk to him, she'd return his call. Otherwise, he'd see her when he returned later this afternoon. He wanted to discuss everything that had happened and ensure she knew nothing had changed in their relationship, at least as far as he was concerned.

Maybe he'd invite her over for dinner tonight so they could get back on better footing. On his return from Alabama, he'd stop at the commissary for a couple steaks to grill.

Things would be better by evening.

At least that's what he hoped.

Becca hoped no one noticed her blotched cheeks or puffy eyes when she returned to CID Headquarters through the rear entrance. She walked the long way around the office skirting Colby's cubicle only to run into Sergeant Otis standing near the fax machine.

"I have to make a phone call, and then I'll stop by Quarters One, Ray, in case anyone asks."

"Anyone like Special Agent Voss, ma'am?"

The sergeant had a knack for putting things together.

"In case you're interested, ma'am, he's driving to Alabama."

"What?"

"Yes, ma'am. Two bodies are being exhumed. He wanted to be there."

Of course he did, without her.

She pushed past Ray, her eyes burning almost as much as her anger.

"Wait up, ma'am. I know you and Agent Voss were working on the explosion investigation. He probably wants you to see this photograph he received from up north. I made a copy for you."

Becca took the file and opened it at her desk. Her heart stopped for a long moment when she looked at the photo. Not of the older woman with the short gray hair and a wide smile, but the man standing behind her.

All the memories came back to haunt her.

She closed the folder and threw it aside, unable to look at the deceitful face that sprouted lies and hate.

A photo she never thought she'd see.

A photo of evil itself.

A photo of Jacob Yoder.

NINETEEN

Becca had to get a grip on herself. She was feeling emotional and needy, which wasn't like her at all. Maybe it was lack of sleep or concern about the investigation or her standing with Chief Wilson. Although more than likely, it was her relationship with Colby.

She's spent too much time this morning stewing over her own mistakes. She needed to buck up and move on. Plus, she needed to contact Mrs. Cameron.

"How can I help you, ma'am?" she asked once the general's wife answered her call.

"I need someone to take the layout of the market stalls to Bishop Zimmerman. Unfortunately, I'm tied up with a Thrift Shop board meeting. The bishop enjoyed talking to you, and I thought you might be able to help me out."

Becca reached for the discarded folder containing Jacob's photo, feeling a sudden burst of energy.

"Yes, ma'am. I'll be glad to deliver the market overview to the bishop."

Hurrying to the copy machine, Becca reproduced Jacob's likeness and dropped a stack of print outs on Sergeant Otis's desk.

"These photos need to be distributed to the military police on post, Ray. Can you let them know Jacob Yoder is a possible suspect in the BOQ explosion?"

"No problem, ma'am, except Special Agent Voss had me email that very same photo to the provost marshal's office so the MPs already have it."

"You talked to Colby?"

"Yes, ma'am. He's still on the road heading to Harmony, Alabama, but he had me notify on-post law enforcement as well the Freemont police who also have the photo. Plus Special Agent Voss put in a be-on-the-lookout order to the Georgia Highway Patrol."

"There's a BOLO out on Jacob Yoder?"

"Yes, ma'am. Anything else you need me to do?"

"No. Thank you, Ray." She turned and headed for the door. "It's seems Special Agent Voss has thought of everything,"

Everything except including her in the investigation.

Becca was mad enough to cry, but she'd already shed too many tears today. Instead, she'd focus on the Amish community and the widow who could be in danger.

Stopping at Quarters One, she picked up the packet containing the plans and layout for the marketplace, and hurried off post. The bishop was cordial when she arrived at his farmhouse. Mrs. Zimmerman invited her inside for a cup of coffee and a piece of pound cake. The offer was tempting, but Becca declined, wanting to talk privately to the bishop.

He walked her to her car and stared into the distance for a long moment before he spoke.

"I talked to Fannie Lehman," he finally said. "The widow had someone helping her. An Amish man from up north. He stayed in her barn for only a few days and is gone now."

"Along with his car?"

The bishop nodded. "That is what she told me."

"Did the widow provide a name?"

"Ezekiel Lapp."

Jacob was using his brother's first name and the new last name he had chosen in Ohio.

"And the dogs?"

"They left with him."

"Was she telling the truth, Bishop?"

"I did not question her honesty. That is something *Gott* will decide."

"She's in danger."

"The widow does not believe he will hurt her."

"You need to warn her. Jacob Yoder is an evil man. He knows how to tempt women. He's killed before. He will kill again."

Becca pulled out a number of copies of Jacob's picture from a folder in her car. "This is his photo. He preys on unsuspecting women, but he has killed others. I suggest you distribute these copies to the Amish families. Make sure Mrs. Lehman sees it as well. I have a strong suspicion this is the man who helped her."

"I do not want violence to upset our way of life. Keep your pictures, Becca. I will pray for God to protect us."

"You'll need more than prayers," Becca insisted. "You need to warn the Amish community, and especially Mrs. Lehman, about Jacob Yoder."

Becca felt a sense of foreboding as she drove away from the bishop's farm. Fannie Lehman was in danger. The bishop, as well as the widow, needed to realize that having a relationship with Jacob Yoder could be deadly.

Becca knew that only too well.

The drive to Harmony seemed especially long and boring. Maybe it was because Colby kept thinking about Becca and wondering how he could mend their broken relationship. He had called her a number of times, but her cell kept going to voice mail.

At least now they had a photo of Jacob Yoder. With a BOLO order in effect, law enforcement across the state would be on high alert for the Amish man and his Crown Vic. Hopefully, he'd be tracked down and brought to justice. That is, if he wasn't buried in the Amish cemetery. There were still too many unanswered questions.

On a whim, Colby had hooked up his GPS, which directed him a new way. He skirted Harmony and drove into a rather expansive subdivision of three- and four-bedroom homes. The community looked comfortable and family friendly and, from the sign on the side of the road, claimed to be a Tucker Reynolds development. Whoever Tucker was, he seemed to be succeeding in this otherwise stagnant economy.

The far end of the housing complex butted up against the Amish community. Colby turned left out of the subdivision and soon spied Lewis and his backhoe. The sheriff's car was parked on the side of the hill along with three other vehicles.

A gathering of men stood watching nearby.

Colby parked and greeted the sheriff.

"There's been a delay with the court order," Lewis said as they shook hands.

"I thought you had the go-ahead."

"The mayor claims exhuming the bodies is a waste of taxpayer money. He's talking to the judge as we speak."

Colby looked around the pristine landscape and the rows of graves, each with a small cement marker. The one near where they stood bore the name Yoder.

"Is there something going on I don't know about? Something more than revenue?"

"The mayor's got his own way of doing things in this town. We've clashed on more than one occasion. In my opinion, he's not interested in what's best for Harmony. His focus is on his construction company and the huge track of homes he's developed and expanded over the years." Lewis pointed in the direction Colby had come.

"I just drove through one of his subdivisions."

Lewis nodded. "His property runs right up against some of the Amish farms. When they go to foreclosure, he makes a phone call to the bank manager, who happens to be a good friend."

"I thought the Amish hold on to their land and pass the farms on to their children," Colby said.

"They try to, but taxes have gone up significantly, and

we had some years of drought. A bad crop can make all the difference for a farmer these days. Plus McDougal's his right-hand man. He likes to threaten the Amish with what could happen."

"McDougal? You mean the former sheriff?"

"One and the same. He started working for Tucker shortly after he retired."

"How does the mayor's interest in real estate have anything to do with the court order?"

"I'm not sure, but if we don't hear from the judge soon, I'll head back to town and talk to him myself."

He looked at Colby. "I could use some backup and would appreciate your support. Having the military involved gives more weight to the situation."

"You've got it."

Lewis pulled out his phone and hit one of the prompts. "Helene, see when I can get in to talk to Judge Clark." He nodded. "Call me back."

A buggy clip-clopped along the nearby road. Colby recognized the woman sitting next to the blond, muscular man leading the horses. Sarah Hershberger. She averted her gaze. Evidently she still hadn't told her husband about Jacob's brother or Colby and Becca's visit.

"Excuse me for a moment." Lewis hustled to where the buggy had stopped on the side of the road. He and the blond man spoke for a few minutes.

"It's Samuel Hershberger," Lewis said when he returned to the gravesite. "You know his wife, Sarah."

Colby nodded. "Did you ever question her about Jacob's brother?"

"Once when she was in town to buy fabric. Samuel wasn't with her, which was fortunate. He might not appreciate a wife who wasn't completely forthright with her husband."

"What did he want today?"

"He asked why we were disturbing the dead."

"Did you tell him?"

Lewis nodded. "He wasn't happy, but then he's carrying a lot of worry, trying to keep afloat and concerned he'll lose the farm."

"More property for the mayor?" Colby asked.

"I hope not. Samuel works as one of our local volunteer firemen to help pay his bills. He's a good man and an asset to the community."

Samuel flicked the reins, and the buggy continued along the road. Sarah glanced back at Colby and nodded her head ever so slightly as if to thank him for keeping her secret.

Lewis's phone rang again. "What'd you find out?" A scowl covered his face. "Not until then?"

He let out a stiff breath. "Okay. Confirm that I'll be there."

He disconnected and turned to Colby. "The judge can't see me until late afternoon. Can you stick around?"

"I'll have to."

But Colby didn't like killing time in Harmony, when he needed to talk to Becca. He tried her cell again and sighed with frustration when she didn't answer.

He'd get back to post too late to see her tonight. Tomorrow was the farmers' market. He would seek her out first thing in the morning, but she'd be busy with security issues. The longer he waited the more likely she wouldn't be interested in listening to what he had to say.

The court order was important, and he'd have to bide his time. Would Becca talk to him when he returned to post? Or was their relationship over before it had even gotten started?

Becca parked in front of Fannie Lehman's house and checked her phone, noticing the missed calls from Colby. As much as she wanted to talk to him, she couldn't. Not now, not until they were face-to-face. She needed to be able to gauge his reaction when she apologized for her actions the other night. She also wanted to question him about leaving her out of the investigation. Of course, Colby was just following Wilson's orders, yet she still felt the sting of humiliation, especially because Colby had been in the chief's office when she'd been counseled on her inappropriate actions. They'd have an opportunity to talk after the investigation was closed and Jacob was brought to justice. Until then, Becca needed to stay away from Colby to protect herself and her heart.

Glancing at the farmhouse, she eased her car door open and listened for the dogs. All she heard was the rustle of the wind in the trees and a few birds who chirped a greeting.

Grabbing one of the printouts from her folder, she stepped to the roadway and flicked her gaze to the barn. Just as before, the door hung open.

No car. No dogs. Hopefully no Jacob Yoder, either.

She climbed the rickety stairs to the front porch and knocked. Once. Twice. Three times.

"Mrs. Lehman, I just came from seeing Bishop Zimmerman. There's something I need to show you."

Evidently the bishop's name pulled weight. The door creaked open. Becca recognized Fannie Lehman as the same woman who had stared at her from the barn raising.

She flashed her identification, introduced herself and shoved the printout in Mrs. Lehman's face before the widow had a chance to reconsider and retreat back into her house.

"Is this the man who was staying here?" Becca asked.

The widow's gaze narrowed. Her hands shook ever so slightly as she stared down at the photo.

"He's dangerous, Mrs. Lehman, and he preys on women living alone."

"Ezekiel is a good man," the widow finally said.

"He's fooling you and trying to win your trust. Then he'll take your valuables and leave you with nothing."

"I do not think this is true."

"You don't have to think, Mrs. Lehman. I know for sure. He's killed women. You are in grave danger. Is there someone you can move in with? Do you have family in the area?"

"I am alone."

"Come with me then. I'll find someplace safe for you to stay?"

The widow shook her head and gave the paper back to Becca. "You must leave now."

"Please listen to me, Mrs. Lehman."

"I have heard you. Now I must prepare my needlework for the market tomorrow."

"You'll be at Fort Rickman in the morning? We can talk more then." Hopefully, the widow would change her mind about accepting help. "I'll contact the Freemont police and ask them to keep your house under surveillance tonight."

If only the widow had a phone or a gun.

"Lock your doors, ma'am, and don't let Jacob—or Ezekiel—in. If you see him, hide until he leaves, then hurry to the bishop's house. He and his wife will help you."

"Do not worry about me, Special Agent Miller. Worry about yourself."

The widow closed the door.

Becca returned to her car, thinking of how easily someone like Jacob could pray upon the Amish. Fannie Lehman wasn't willing to accept help. That self-sufficiently had probably been drummed into her since she was a little girl.

Glancing back, she saw the curtain move ever so slightly and knew the widow was watching.

The older woman had a mind of her own.

Independence or stupidity?

Becca wasn't sure, but one thing was certain. She and Fannie were a lot alike.

TWENTY

Saturday dawned cold and damp, not the ideal setting for the first farmers' market and craft fair. Mrs. Cameron had hoped for blue skies and sunshine, but even the general's wife couldn't control the weather.

Becca's mood matched the gray sky. She had slept little if at all. Her thoughts had been on Colby and the way she felt wrapped in his embrace. Not that she would ever know that feeling again. Anything that might have developed was over between them, no matter how much she wished otherwise.

Her heart was heavy when she arrived at the grassy knoll ahead of schedule. Located near the Fort Rickman Museum and nearby river, the expansive area was filled with newly erected booths, all painted white.

Many of the Amish families had already arrived in their buggies. The horses and rigs were in a special spot behind the cordoned-off site reserved for automobile parking.

The military had provided trucks and transported the larger items for sale. Finely designed tables and benches stood near dollhouses and rocking chairs. The Amish men had arranged the pieces for display while the women hung beautiful quilts and crocheted lap blankets in the various stalls.

In other booths, spring cuttings and winter vegetables sat next to Mason jars filled with colorful jams and jellies.

An assortment of homemade breads and cakes and pies made Becca's mouth water as she walked around the perimeter of the market and examined the wares. She bought a cinnamon roll that melted in her mouth and washed it down with a cup of coffee the Army Community Services was selling to raise money for some of their on-post programs.

Slowly the area started to come alive as more people from both the *English* and Amish communities arrived. From what Becca could tell, the committee members spearheading the event handled their jobs with great attention to detail, and the day promised to be a success in spite of the less than perfect weather.

Becca briefed the military police she had requested to help with security and passed out copies of Jacob's photograph. Although she wanted everyone to know who to be watching for in the crowd, she also stressed the importance of maintaining good relationships with the Amish. Her final instruction was to check with her before confronting anyone who might fit Jacob's description.

Glancing at her watch, she stamped her feet against the chill. The earth was damp with dew, and a breeze tugged at her jacket. At least she had donned slacks and a heavy sweater.

Colby was probably still in his BOQ, catching a few extra winks of shut-eye this Saturday morning. Maybe he would appear later, although she almost hoped he wouldn't. She had a job to do and didn't want to be distracted by the handsome agent who had woven his way into her heart.

As much as Becca wanted to apologize for her actions, she knew the night before last had been a turning point. Maybe a stopping point would be a better term to use. Colby had been perfectly clear that he wanted to keep everything professional. He was right, of course, yet she still regretted what had happened. Even more than that, she regretted losing Colby.

Mrs. Cameron approached her. "Everything seems to be going as planned, Becca. The security team has been most helpful, and I'm sure we won't have any problems today."

"That's my hope, ma'am. What time is General Cameron planning to arrive?"

"His opening remarks are scheduled for nine. He had

some papers to sign at his office, but I'm sure he'll be here soon. The band's getting ready to warm up, and the children's choir from the Main Post Chapel is on its way."

"You've done a great job with all the details, ma'am."

The senior wife smiled. "It was everyone coming together to help make it happen. I'm so glad you could be part of the committee."

"Thank you, ma'am. We'll keep our eyes open and wait until the day's over before we let down our guard."

"I'm relieved to know you're here, Becca. Now, if you'll excuse me, I want to buy a quilt for the guest bedroom. Bishop Zimmerman said his wife had some lovely patterns that I might like."

Mrs. Cameron hurried to a booth where a number of bed-coverings hung over the wooden frame. The bishop stood nearby and watched the two women examine the various quilts, all colorful patterns Becca knew so well.

The band started to play a jaunty march, and soon people were tapping their feet or clapping their hands to the music.

As if with new eyes, Becca saw the beauty of the Amish way of accepting each day as a gift from God. In her youth, she had wanted to control her own life, something with which she still struggled, but as she glanced around the marketplace, she was overcome with a renewed appreciation for these good people who put God first. If only she could share this bit from her past with Colby.

She circled through the area and was relieved to see Fannie Lehman arranging handmade aprons and crocheted shawls in one of the rear stalls. Noticing the woman's furtive glance over her shoulder and the dark lines that circled her eyes, Becca hurried forward.

"Is something wrong?" she asked, her own gaze flicking to the nearby parking area. "Did Jacob Yoder come back?"

The widow hung her head.

Becca reached out to touch her hand. Fannie glanced up. The look on her face spoke volumes about her struggle.

"Is he here?" Becca asked again.

The older woman pursed her lips as if annoyed. "I told you he left the area."

"You don't have to be afraid," Becca insisted. "I'll be close by. If you see him, let me know. A number of military police are in the crowd. We won't let him hurt you."

"I do not fear for myself."

"Is there someone else he wants to harm?"

The woman looked into Becca's eyes. "I thought you knew. He wants to hurt you."

General Cameron arrived at the fair shortly before nine. The two stars on the general's flag flying from the front bumper of his sedan looked impressive, and many of the shoppers turned to stare as he climbed from the car.

His aide rode with the general and escorted him to the stage area. Mrs. Cameron met him there. Together they walked to where the bishop stood. The men shook hands and chatted amicably before the general nodded and pointed to the stage. He and Mrs. Cameron climbed the raised platform and approached the podium.

Becca glanced back at the widow's stall to ensure Fannie Lehman was all right.

Her heart jerked in her chest.

The booth was empty.

She circled through the crowd. The general's voice boomed over the loudspeaker.

"Welcome to the first annual farmers' market and craft fair hosted by Fort Rickman and our new Freemont neighbors in the Amish community."

Becca flicked her gaze to the surrounding stalls. Surely the widow was talking to a friend. Perhaps she had gone for a cup of coffee.

Glancing at the beverage stand, Becca's optimism plummeted. A young woman and her two little ones were the only customers in line.

To the right of the stage, the bishop and his wife stood. Just like many of the other people, their attention was focused on the general.

Becca's neck tensed. Where was Fannie Lehman?

She raised her cell and called the head MP onsite. "I'm looking for the Amish woman who was in stall seventeen. Gray hair, about 145 pounds, five feet four inches. She was wearing a blue dress, apron and a short black jacket."

"Ah, we've got a problem, ma'am. I see a number of Amish women who fit that description."

"Jacob Yoder might be in the crowd. Inform your men. Let's search the area. If you see anything, call me."

She disconnected, wishing Colby were here. He would understand the urgency in finding the widow and ensuring she was okay.

Becca hurried to the widow's stall and peered behind the counter. Seeing nothing out of order, she checked the surrounding booths.

Cars filled the designated parking area. The horses and rigs were lined up in the distance. Perhaps Fannie had gone back to her buggy. Becca double-timed across the field.

Behind her, the general continued to talk about how the military and civilians in Freemont had come together on a number of projects. Both he and Mrs. Cameron hoped today's market would grow into a bimonthly event that would draw people from the outlining areas.

Cheers from the crowd punctuated his pauses as he introduced the Freemont mayor and city council.

Becca neared the first buggy and gazed into the carriage, seeing nothing except a lap blanket neatly folded on the seat.

A horse neighed. She turned at the sound and saw something on the grass. A quilt or—

The widow.

She raced to where Fannie lay. Becca felt her neck relieved to find a pulse.

A bulging welt on the woman's forehead and scratches to her throat confirmed the foul play Becca suspected. Raising her cell, she called the MP with whom she had just spoken.

Before she could say anything, a rag covered her nose and mouth. "No," she tried to scream, inhaling a sickening sweet smell that affected her equilibrium. She fought against the cloying scent and the hands and the body that overpowered her.

Her strength ebbed. The scream died in her throat, and slowly the world turned dark as she pitched forward onto the cold, damp grass.

Colby pulled into the parking lot of the farmers' market much later than he had hoped after being tied up at CID Headquarters with Chief Wilson. The general had concluded his remarks and a group of schoolchildren were taking the stage.

Exiting his car, Colby's gut tightened as he spied four MPs gathered in the rear of the whitewashed stalls. He glanced around the area, looking for Becca. Fear settled along his spine. Something had happened and it wasn't good.

Racing toward the men, he held up his identification. "CID. Where's Special Agent Miller?"

A corporal, tall and beefy, shook his head. "That's what we want to know. I got a call from her, but she didn't say anything. I only heard a gasp."

Colby's heart lurched. "How long ago?"

The corporal raised his cell. "The call came in ten minutes ago."

"Fan out. Check the parking area." Colby pointed to a second MP. "Call your headquarters for backup."

"Over here." A young Amish woman waved frantically

from where the buggies were parked. "Fannie's hurt. I need help."

Colby called CID Headquarters as he raced forward. Ray Otis answered. "I need an ambulance and every available CID agent at the market area. Agent Miller is missing. Lock down the post. Set up roadblocks. We could be looking for a 2005 Crown Vic, metallic blue, or an Amish buggy. Search each car leaving post."

"Roger that. I'm on it."

"She's hurt her head," the young woman told Colby as he approached, noting the angry lump on the older woman's forehead and the marks on her neck.

He knelt and felt for a pulse. "An ambulance is on the way." He turned to glance at the nearby road. "Did you see anyone leaving the area?"

She shook her head. "No."

One of the MPs approached.

"Stay here until the EMTs arrive," Colby ordered.

He raised his cell again. "Ray, have the river path checked. Someone could have escaped along that route unnoticed."

"Will do, sir. I contacted the guardhouse at the main gate. An Amish buggy passed through not more than two minutes ago."

"Call the Freemont police. Have them set up roadblocks. We need to stop that buggy."

Hearing the sirens approach, Colby left the MP in charge of the widow's care and hurried back to his car.

He pulled onto the main road and accelerated, stopping only briefly at the Main Gate.

"Which direction did the buggy go?" he asked the guard on duty.

"North, sir, toward Freemont."

A horse-drawn carriage could never outrun a motorized

vehicle. Colby pressed down on the accelerator. Fear tangled through his gut.

Jacob Yoder was on the loose and he had Becca.

Colby had to find her before it was too late.

TWENTY-ONE

Becca's head throbbed, and her muscles ached as if she had the flu. Blinking her eyes open, she knew any illness would have been better than what she faced.

Her hands and legs were tied, and she was lying on a dirty mattress, wedged against the wall. She raised her head and stared around the small, bare room. A jackhammer of pain stuttered through her skull.

She moaned.

As if in response, a dog growled. His paws tap-danced across the wooden floor. She smelled the animal before she saw him. A huge, black beast with pointed ears and large jowls.

The Doberman she had seen at the widow's house.

A second dog trotted forward, larger than the first. A female. She barked twice.

A door creaked. Afraid to turn, Becca kept her gaze on the animals. The shuffle of footsteps approached the bed.

"You're awake." Jacob's voice.

"Call off the dogs." Becca tried to sound assertive.

"You're frightened by them?"

He knew she was.

"Because of your father's threats about the neighbor's dog. Is that not right?"

She refused to respond.

"All right, Rebecca. Hearing your voice after all these years has softened my heart. I will do as you ask." He snapped his fingers and the dogs backed off.

Becca let out the breath she had been holding and dropped her head onto the thin mattress. The musty smell filled her nostrils and sickened her stomach.

Jacob peered down into her line of view.

Again her stomach rolled.

His eyes were wide and a smirk covered his mouth. "You haven't changed, Rebecca."

"I've gotten smarter."

He sneered. "Not smart enough to run from me."

She didn't answer. He was right. She'd allowed herself to get caught.

"I've missed you." His voice had a seductive pull that sent another volley of fear to weave around her spine.

"You've been busy, Jacob, wooing unsuspecting older women. You used them and killed them and ran off with their money and their treasures." She steeled herself to act defiant.

"You don't know where I've been or what I've done."

"I know you killed your mother."

His face twisted with rage. He raised his hand and slapped her face. Her head crashed against the wall. Pain like white lightning shot through her.

"No," she cried, unable to control herself.

"Did you like that? Because that's what my mother used to do to me. My brother, Ezekiel, and I tried to run away from her, but she always found us. I never complained and suffered in silence. Do you know about that, Rebecca? Do you know how to suffer in silence?"

"You killed your brother and your wife and then burned down the house around them."

He shook his head. "Ezekiel died so that I might live."

"Are you parsing words, Jacob. Do you even understand what that means?"

"If you think I am *doppick,* dumb, why did you fall in love with me?"

The question Becca had struggled with for so long. Coming face-to-face with him after all this time allowed her to see more clearly. She hadn't been at fault. Jacob had wooed her just as he wooed the widows.

"I was young and foolish and taken by an older man who promised to show me the world."

"Yet you changed, Rebecca."

"You mean after you married Mary and still tried to have your way with me."

He laughed. His hand touched a lock of her hair. "You fought so hard, even when I surprised you in the barn. I knew your father would not believe you. He thought you tried to seduce me, didn't he?" Jacob chuckled. "Your father loved you, but he loved money more."

"My father saw what he wanted to see. He thought you were a good man. How completely you fooled him, Jacob."

"I told you not to run from me, Rebecca. I said how mad I got when people left me. Katie promised not to leave me, but she went home to pack a bag just as you had done the night I said I'd meet you at the covered bridge."

"Thankfully you never showed up because you were already laying claim to the widow Mary."

"Merely investing in our future. The farm was worth saving, which you didn't understand."

"I understood about Mary's failing health. You poisoned her."

He shook his head and laughed. "I provided relief from her aches and pains. She was old and infirmed when I married her. Since I couldn't have you, I wanted Katie, but she rejected me just as you had done."

"You killed her because she tried to escape." Anger mixed with Becca's fear. "Katie called me from Elizabeth's house and said she needed help. I didn't want Elizabeth to get hurt so I told Katie to go home, thinking my father would protect her until I arrived. Only you got there first."

Overcome with the guilt she still carried because she had sent Katie home to her death, Becca moaned.

"You're an animal, Jacob." She glanced at his dogs. "Although that's an insult to your pups."

He put his hands over his ears like a child. The sleeve of his shirt slipped down, exposing red welts on his arms.

"Does it bother you to hear the truth?" she pressed, thinking of Elizabeth and how she had fought to save herself.

He backed from the bed and pulled a bottle from a shelf in the corner, but she continued on.

"You killed Katie and my father and Elizabeth Konig and your wife and brother and mother. An Amish woman died in Tennessee and an *English* widow in Kentucky. You're planning to kill Fannie Lehman and me and probably more people until someone stops you."

She saw the rag in his hand and scooted closer to the wall, trying to distance herself from Jacob and the chloroform.

"No." She shook her head.

He glanced at the animals lying in the corner and nodded. Both dogs trotted to where he stood.

"The dogs won't hurt unless you try to escape. In that case, they will attack you. The last person they stopped did not survive." He leaned closer. She smelled his stale breath and saw the evil in his eyes. "You won't be able to run ever again."

He lowered the cloth to her face. She struggled, trying to free herself from the restraints and from the saturated rag that covered her nose. She held her breath far too long and gasped when her lungs were ready to burst.

Instead of air, she inhaled the chloroform that took her to another place far from Jacob Yoder and his dogs.

Colby raced along the Georgia back roads that skirted Freemont and led to the Amish community. He passed a number of farms and turned onto the narrow path that ran through the forested area.

At the clearing, he pulled to the side of the road, drew

his weapon and ran toward the Lehman widow's house. He pushed through the door, surprised to find it unlocked, and moved stealthily from room to room.

Finding nothing that had bearing on where Jacob had taken Becca, he climbed the stairs, his senses on high alert and his weapon raised to fend off any attack. At the second-floor landing, he turned into the long hallway and made his way from room to room.

Once outside, he hurried to the barn and pulled the door open. Empty.

He studied the landscape. Even the dogs were gone. The widow was in the hospital. A phone call from Ray said she had revealed nothing they didn't already know.

Colby hurried back to his car.

Where was Becca and how would he find her?

The door creaked open. Becca kept her eyes shut, hoping Jacob would think she was still drugged.

"Hey, pups."

She was sickened by the irony of a man who killed in cold blood yet cared so lovingly for his dogs. Their paws brushed against the floor as they danced around their master.

Footsteps approached the bed. She could feel his presence and knew he was peering down at her.

Don't move.

Don't react to his nearness.

Think of better days.

A mental image came to mind. Colby standing next to her. His hand on her arm.

The thought soothed her fear and brought comfort.

"Rebecca?" Jacob touched her cheek. She struggled not to recoil. "You are still asleep?"

He turned and called the dogs. They scurried forward.

Their cool, moist snouts nuzzled her face, sending waves of repulsion rippling through her.

She fisted her hands tied behind her. Her nails dug into her flesh.

"Come, pups."

Evidently satisfied she was still drugged, Jacob's footsteps moved toward the door. The dogs whined.

"Yes, yes. We will take a walk while Rebecca sleeps."

The door opened, then closed. Silence filled the void.

Becca's eyes popped open. Her gaze flitted around the room. The bottle of chloroform sat on a wall shelf. No pictures. No curtain at the small window above the bed.

She strained against the ropes binding her hands and feet. Scooting to the side of the mattress, she forced her legs over the edge and pulled herself upright.

Her head pounded in protest, and she closed her eyes to the kaleidoscope of light exploding through her brain. Her stomach rumbled, and a wave of nausea forced her to drop her head and take deep breaths.

Something sharp jabbed the back of her leg.

She shifted to see more clearly. A raw edge extended from the bedframe.

She shimmied closer and twisted her hands until they touched the exposed metal. Would the edge be sharp enough?

Slowly, deliberately, she rubbed the rope against the roughness. Concentrating, she added force to each thrust. A portion of the thick hemp frayed loose. She groaned and tugged at the restraints, unable to break free.

She expected to hear Jacob's voice or the barking dogs. Silence.

Returning to the task, she continued to saw the rope. Back and forth. Back and forth.

The metal nicked her hand. She grimaced but refused to stop. Every second was precious. She had to keep working to free herself.

Over and over again, she sliced at the remaining portion of cord. With one last thrust, the rope gave way.

Gasping with relief, she rubbed her wrists. Her shoulders ached. Leaning forward, she untied her legs and wobbled as she tried to stand. The room shifted. She hesitated and then stumbled to the door.

Opening it ever so slowly, she peered into the living area of the small cabin. Couch, card table and folding chair. Frayed, braided rug lay in front of the fireplace. Small kitchen area to the left.

Two doors. One beside the front window, the other next to the kitchen stove.

Gathering her courage, she lifted up a silent prayer. *Please, Lord, keep me safe.*

She hurried across the room and cracked the back door, seeing low hills and the end of a gravel driveway.

Stepping onto the small stoop, she breathed in the cool, fresh air. Her gaze flicked right, left.

A thick wooded area sat forty feet behind the cabin. She ran. Her legs ached and her head pounded. She tripped over a mound of dirt and nearly toppled forward.

Still sluggish from the chloroform, she stumbled again but pushed on. She had to keep moving. Eventually she would come to a road or a house or someone who could help her.

Ten feet farther and she'd disappear into the thick underbrush. Jacob would never find her there.

The sound came with the wind and sent terror through her veins.

"No, please."

Her blood chilled.

She glanced over her shoulder, knowing what was behind her.

Gaining…

Closing in…

She heard them…

The dogs.

TWENTY-TWO

Colby joined Wilson in the CID Headquarters conference room where special agents and staff personnel were studying maps, plugging coordinates into laptops and relaying information to other law enforcement agencies around the state.

Wilson looked as worried as Colby felt.

"Don Palmer from the Freemont PD is compiling information on any abandoned cabins, caves, anyplace Yoder might be hiding," the chief said. "We've been doing a similar search with maps and satellite images of the surrounding areas. The Highway Patrol in Georgia and all neighboring states have photos of Yoder and Becca and are on the lookout for a blue Crown Vic. All county sheriff offices and police departments have also been notified."

Which still wasn't enough.

Colby checked his watch. Time was passing too quickly, and they were no closer to finding Becca.

Glancing at the maps strewn over the conference table, Colby tried to concentrate on what he knew about Jacob and his past. Amish communities. Rural locales. Isolated farms.

Something niggled in the back of his mind. What was it? If only he could remember.

Frustrated, Colby stepped into the hallway and headed to his cubicle. He glanced at the list of Amish communities and police departments still on his desk. A list Becca had compiled.

Rubbing his hand across his forehead, he groaned. *Please, Lord. Lead me to her.*

What had he heard or seen recently about a remote hunting cabin?

Rifling through the papers on his desk, he stumbled on

the photo of Jacob Yoder attached to the printout of the Kentucky widow's property. Scanning the items from her estate, he felt a surge of euphoria and tapped in the number for the sheriff's office.

"I need Stan Oaks," he said after hastily stating his name and affiliation.

"He's not here, sir."

"Where is he?"

"In the hospital. Possible appendectomy."

Colby's stomach tightened and not with sympathy. "He mentioned a widow who died some months ago. Lucy Reynolds. She owned a cabin in Alabama."

"I can check on that, sir."

Colby shoved the phone closer to his ear.

He needed to get in his car and drive. He didn't know where. Staying in the office made him want to scream.

"Sir," the deputy came back on the line.

"Did you find the cabin's location?"

"I'm not sure, sir. There's mention of a place over the state line from Georgia. I checked the map. It's north of Dothan and west of Eufaula."

Colby raced back to the conference room. Wilson looked up when he reached for the Alabama map and spread it over the table.

"Where's the cabin in relation to Harmony, Alabama?" Colby asked the deputy, the phone still at his ear.

"It on a rural route, sir. Looks to be southeast of Harmony by about thirty or forty miles." He provided the address. Colby wrote it on a scrap of paper and handed it to Wilson.

The chief plugged the address into the satellite search. A shabby cabin came into view.

Colby went with his gut and his gut screamed Becca.

"I need a chopper."

"You've got it." Wilson picked up his own phone and contacted the aviation unit on post.

"They'll be ready to lift off as soon as you arrive at the airfield."

"Call Alabama Highway Patrol," Colby ordered. "I'll contact Lewis Stone in Harmony. We'll rendezvous at the cabin. Whoever gets there first needs to call me."

He left without uttering another word. Time was running out. He had to find Becca.

Becca woke and blinked her eyes. Her head throbbed. She moaned, remembering the dogs that had surrounded her and Jacob's hand crashing against her ear.

He'd dragged her screaming and kicking to the cabin for another dose of chloroform that sent her into a chilling darkness where she'd confronted killer canines that attacked without mercy.

Hallucinations from the drug, no doubt, yet the attacks had seemed so real. She shivered at the memory and opened her eyes, needing to ground herself in reality. Four bare walls. Two Dobermans by the door. The chloroform cloth, near the bed, as if Jacob had dropped it on his way out the door.

"Give yourself up, Yoder."

The blare of a bullhorn sounded through the stillness. A similar voice had bellowed in her dreams. The warnings hadn't been her imagination.

She wanted to rejoice, but everything could go south fast, especially with a volatile psychopath like Jacob calling the shots.

Becca moved her legs and arms. She wasn't bound. Had law enforcement arrived before Jacob could tie her up again?

Overhead the *whomp, whomp, whomp* of the rotor blades of a helicopter cut through the air. The roar of the craft grew more intense. Wind blew the trees. Somewhere close by, the chopper touched down.

The dogs clawed at the door and whined.

In one swift move, she reached for the dropped rag and jammed it in her pocket. Having to search for a new cloth would cause Jacob aggravation and buy her time.

Another volley of pain. She clamped down on her jaw, unwilling to distract the dogs and draw attention to herself.

The door creaked open. She shut her eyes and inwardly groaned, expecting Jacob to approach the bed. She'd fight him to the death this time. Although weak as she was and still reeling from the effects of the chloroform, the odds would be overwhelmingly in his favor. Even without adding the Dobermans to the mix.

The door closed.

She raised her head.

No dogs.

She dropped her feet to the ground and stood. The room went black. Lowering her head, she grimaced until the vertigo passed.

Twilight was falling outside, and long shadows filled the narrow room.

Hurry, an inner voice warned.

She stumbled to the window. Small though it was, she unlatched the lock and pushed on the glass that refused to budge. Drawing on her reserves, she tried again with the same result. Breaking the window would alert Jacob. Still, it was an option, and she didn't have many at this point.

She glanced around the barren room and reached for the chloroform bottle on the shelf, unsure if it be heavy enough to break the glass.

"We know you're holding Special Agent Miller." The bullhorn again. "Let her go, Yoder."

The shuffle of feet.

The dogs barked just outside the door. Jacob was coming. *Think. Think.*

She dumped chloroform on the rag and backed against the wall. If only he wouldn't see her there.

The door opened. Jacob stepped into the room.

Becca jumped him from behind and jammed the rag against his nose.

His elbow jabbed her gut. Air wheezed from her lungs. He grabbed her wrist and turned until he had her in a rear choke hold with her right arm angled up against her spine. Pain radiated across her shoulder.

The dogs growled.

She kicked her foot back, hoping to make contact with Jacob's shin. He sidestepped. His hold around on her neck tightened.

He forced her forward. "You're coming with me."

She shook her head. "Let me go, Jacob. You can't escape now."

Half pushing, half dragging, he shoved her into the main room.

She kicked again, then locked her knees.

Enraged, he increased the tension on her wrist. Tears stung her eye. Sure that he'd rip her arm from its socket, she arched her back and moved forward.

He pushed her toward the window by the front door and smashed her face against the cool glass. Patrol cars from every agency—local police, county sheriff's office, state highway patrol—were parked along the dirt road.

Crushing her with his weight, he raised a gun to her head, cracked the front door and screamed through the opening. "You shoot and Rebecca dies."

She tried to fight him, but he was too big and too powerful. She needed help.

Glancing into the falling darkness, she searched for a face she knew. Someone she had pushed away forty-eight hours earlier because of her own fear. She hadn't wanted to expose the past, but it had found her just as Jacob had.

She saw him in the sea of uniforms.

Colby.

* * *

Colby's heart lurched. He couldn't take his eyes off Becca's twisted face shoved against the windowpane. Jacob was a killer and a maniac. At least she was alive, although Colby could only imagine what she'd endured.

He fisted his hands and swallowed the angry bile that filled his throat. From the beginning, Becca had insisted Jacob was seeking revenge. She'd been right. Now she was paying for law enforcement's inability to accept what she had told them all along.

A county deputy had been first on the scene. He'd called Lewis Stone who had driven here from Harmony. Thankfully, the sheriff had contacted Colby, although getting confirmation Jacob had captured Becca felt like a sucker punch to his gut. He'd wanted to double over in pain. Instead he formed a plan, seeing the layout of the cabin in his mind from the satellite imaging.

Jacob wanted freedom and a safe passage out of the country. Lewis had been negotiating with him over the phone. They'd switched to the bullhorn to let Becca know she wasn't alone.

As soon as the military chopper had touched down, Colby assessed the situation and looked for a way to get inside the cabin. The side window was too small, leaving the back door as the best option.

"I'm going in," Colby told the Harmony sheriff.

"Wait until dark."

"There's no time. Jacob's irrational and escalating."

"We'll go in together," Lewis insisted.

Colby held up his hand. "Stay on the bullhorn. He knows your voice. Keep him calm and agree to anything he wants."

"He wants a new car and a new life in Canada."

"Convince him everything will be forgiven if he doesn't harm Becca."

"That's what I keep promising him."

Would it be enough?

The sound of an approaching car caused both men to glance over their shoulders. Frank McDougal, the former county sheriff, sat behind the wheel.

Riding shotgun was a man Colby had met last night—and instantly disliked—when he and Lewis had tried unsuccessfully to convince the judge to sign the exhumation order.

Tucker Reynolds. Harmony's mayor was as pompous as he was large and flaunted his wealth along with his ego.

Colby's stomach soured. "What's Tucker doing here?"

Lewis shook his head. "Probably another attempt to shove his weight around. Don't let him throw you. I'll handle the mayor and McDougal."

Colby nodded. "Give me three minutes to get in place." They both glanced at their watches.

"Where's that new car you promised me?" Jacob shouted from inside the house.

Lewis grabbed Colby's arm. "You need a vest."

Even at this distance, he saw the fear in Becca's eyes. "There's no time. Remember three minutes. Keep Jacob occupied."

Colby disappeared into the nearby stand of trees and made his way to the side of the cabin. He peered through the small window and saw the empty room. Continuing around the house, he approached the back door.

"Lord, let it be unlocked."

"The car's on the way." Lewis's voice over the bullhorn. "How much cash will you need, Yoder?"

Colby hesitated. Would Jacob take the bait or realize he was being set up?

"Five thousand," he called back.

Colby nodded. A small, but significant step in the right direction.

Lewis had been confident he could negotiate Becca's freedom. Colby wanted a more hands-on approach. He didn't trust Jacob, and waiting until nightfall would provide an opportunity for him to slip away under the cover of darkness.

"What denomination of bills?" Lewis again.

Colby glanced at his watch and counted down the remaining seconds. Three. Two. One.

Pulling in a deep breath, he turned the doorknob ever so slowly.

TWENTY-THREE

Becca had felt a surge of relief when she first saw Colby outside the cabin. Now she couldn't find him in the crowd of uniformed personnel.

Hopefully he wasn't doing something foolish like trying to be a hero. *Please, Lord, keep him safe.*

She saw Frank McDougal raise the trunk of his car. Strange for him to be on-site.

An overweight guy in a coat and tie slouched against the hood of the same car, looking somewhat bored.

Another blast from the bullhorn. "We'll stock the car with food and water, Yoder."

"You'll be free, Jacob." She tried to sound confident and keep the fear from her voice.

"I do not trust them," he grumbled. "They will kill me if I let you go."

"That's not true."

"I told you before, Rebecca. You will never run from me again."

Lewis raised the bullhorn. "Is there anything else you need, Yoder?"

Jacob lowered his mouth to her ear. His stale breath fanned her cheek. "I need you."

She had to let Jacob think he was in control.

"I'll go with you willingly." She softened her voice and relaxed against him. "I was wrong before. Now I see more clearly. You had to endure so much. I ran away. No wonder you were angry with me."

He eased his hold on her ever so slightly. "I cannot forgive you, Rebecca."

"Of course not. I hurt you just as Katie did, but I can make it up to you."

"You are lying. My mother told me I was bad when I ran away, like my father had done. She said no one would love me or want to be with me."

"That's not true."

Becca glanced behind her, searching for the dogs. Jacob had let down his guard. She needed to act.

Seeing movement out of the corner of her eye, Becca peered into the shadows, knowing instinctively she had seen something.

She had seen Colby.

Standing in the open doorway, Colby quickly assessed his options. None of them was good with Becca in the line of fire.

Jacob stood behind her, a .38 special jammed against her head. The only hope was to provide a distraction.

As if sensing his presence, Becca nodded almost imperceptibly then jammed her heel onto Jacob's instep.

He cursed and lifted his injured foot.

She dropped like a dead weight, forcing him off balance. Twisting out of his grasp, she fell to the floor and rolled.

Colby raised his gun. Before he could fire, a dog lunged from out of nowhere. Razor-sharp teeth sank into his arm.

"Aah!" He fought to free himself.

Another dog grabbed his leg.

Becca screamed.

The gun slipped from Colby's hand.

Two tear-gas canisters sailed through the front door, landing on the frayed rug.

Smoke and flame billowed from the incendiary devices.

The weight of the dogs knocked Colby to the floor. He

fought to free his arms, his legs. They were on him, over him, growling, biting, tearing at his flesh.

His only thought was Becca.

The threadbare rug caught fire. Smoke and tear gas mixed into a deadly combination.

Becca's heart stopped.

Colby lay on the floor, overpowered by the savage Dobermans. His gun out of reach.

One of the dogs backed into the fire and yelped.

He threw his weight and flipped the other Doberman onto his back. The dog pawed the air. Colby righted himself, and both animals ran yipping out the back door.

Jacob coughed and rubbed his eyes. Then, as if in slow motion, he raised his gun and took aim.

In half a heartbeat Colby would be dead, killed by the man who had taken everyone Becca had ever loved.

Ignoring the caustic tear gas that burned her throat, she groped along the floor, unable to find Colby's gun. *Please, God!*

Her fingers wrapped around the grip. Using two hands, she raised the weapon and squeezed the trigger.

Jacob gasped as the bullet pierced his chest. His eyes widened. He stared at her through the smoky haze. Disbelief washed over his face. He fell to his knees and crumbled chest-first onto the floor.

His blood, dark and thick, spilled across the hardwood planks just as her father's blood had done so long ago.

Before she could process what had happened, Colby was lifting her, holding her, running with her to safety.

TWENTY-FOUR

Colby ushered Becca from the smoke-filled cabin into the still-remaining daylight. He pulled her close and stared into her eyes, needing to ensure she was all right. "Did he hurt you?"

She shook her head and nestled against his chest. "I'm okay."

All around them cops raced into the cabin. Jacob was dragged outside. He was alive, but only barely. EMTs worked to save him.

Firemen poured water on the blaze. The smell of smoke and tear gas filled the air.

The dogs were found and tranquilized then carted off to the pound.

Additional medical personnel approached Colby. "We'll need to treat those bites, sir."

He held up his hand, unwilling to move away from Becca. "Give me a minute."

Lewis raced forward. "You two okay?"

Colby nodded. "Who tossed the gas?"

"McDougal. I thought you made the request."

"No, but it may have saved our lives."

"You should thank him," Becca suggested, easing from his arms.

"Good idea." Colby spied the former sheriff heading to his car and hustled toward him.

"Wait up, McDougal."

"Nice job, Colby." He laughed nervously. A muscle twitched in his neck. "That's one dude who needed to be taken down."

Confused by the former sheriff's comment as well as his

unease, Colby thought back to what he knew about the case. Slowly one of the missing pieces fell into place.

"Funny," Colby said, sauntering closer, "that you didn't ask who was in the cabin since you buried Jacob eight years ago."

McDougal quickly shooed off the remark. "The body was badly burned. Of course, I thought it was Jacob back then. Who else would have been in Yoder's house?"

"His brother, Ezekiel, was visiting. What a shame you jumped to the wrong conclusion. Or was there a reason you said Jacob had died in the fire?"

Colby spied the mayor backtracking into the crowd. "Where're you going, Tucker? Back to Harmony to buy more land?"

The mayor grumbled. "What are you talking about?"

"I'm talking about the Yoder property. You needed another entrance into your mega subdivision. The widow Mary's farm was headed for foreclosure until Jacob took up with her. He turned the farm around, but you still wanted the land. That's why McDougal had to claim Jacob's body was recovered in the fire, so you could buy the property after the estate went to probate."

The mayor's eyes widened. "That's preposterous."

Samuel Hershberger, wearing his volunteer firefighter shirt open over his black pants and suspenders, stepped from the crowd of law enforcement personnel and first responders. "Jacob Yoder was my neighbor. His was not the body I pulled from the fire that night long ago."

Lewis patted McDougal's shoulder. "You knew the body you uncovered wasn't Jacob's, which means you falsified official documents. We need to have a talk."

On the way to the squad car, the sheriff pointed to the mayor. "I know where to find you, Tucker. Don't leave town."

Colby glanced at the ambulance. EMTs were still hovering over the stretcher where Jacob lay.

One of the paramedics approached Becca. "Yoder's calling for you, ma'am. He's agitated. Might calm him a bit if you'd talk to him. He keeps saying *Mamm, Mamm.*"

"That's Pennsylvania Dutch. He's calling for his mother." She glanced at Colby.

"I'll go with you," he assured her.

She hesitated a moment and then nodded. Together they walked to the stretcher.

Jacob raised his head. His eyes were wild with fear, his lips dry and caked with blood.

"I…I'm sorry." He grabbed Becca's arm. "For…give… me, *Mamm.*"

Jacob thought she was his mother. He was dying and wanted forgiveness, yet he had killed everyone Becca loved. How could she forgive him?

She stared down at Jacob for a long moment then her gaze softened as if the weight that she had carried for too long had eased.

She pulled in a deep breath and patted Jacob's hand.

"I…I forgive you, Jacob."

"It's over." Becca stepped into Colby's arms as the ambulance pulled away.

Law enforcement still had more to do at the crime scene, and cops hustled back and forth between their squad cars and the cabin.

Looking up at him, she sighed. "I need to apologize for Thursday night. I gave my heart too readily when Jacob first came into my life and carried that burden, along with feeling responsible for Katie's death. I told her to wait for me at home that night, otherwise she might have been safe staying with Elizabeth. I was afraid your questions would force me to reveal my own guilt."

"Oh, honey, it wasn't your fault that Katie died. You're not to blame," he insisted.

Becca nodded ever so slightly. "I'm beginning to realize that you're right, but I still shouldn't have gotten upset with you."

He touched her chin and tilted her head back so he could see into her beautiful eyes that made him forget about killers and attack dogs.

"I thought I'd lost you that night, Becca, in one way, and then today I thought I'd lost you for good."

"Oh, Colby, I tried to take care of myself—only I needed you. Just as I needed God when I shut Him out. My *datt* said I had a problem with pride."

"Your father had the problem. How could he not be proud of you, Becca? You're the most wonderful person I've ever met. You're beautiful and determined and strong and committed to doing what's right. I grew up surrounded by love and you had no one. Yet what you did for Jacob taught me about forgiveness and compassion. Jacob took everything from you. I don't know how you could forgive him."

"I had to or my heart would have turned as dark as his. I thought about the lessons I heard each Sunday as a child, about God's forgiveness and his love, about everlasting life and salvation. I now see the goodness of the Amish way that I turned my back on years ago."

He pulled her closer. "I love you, Rebecca Meuller and Becca Miller, whichever name you choose."

His smile faded replaced with an intensity he hadn't expected. "I'd like you to take my name someday."

"Oh, Colby."

He touched his finger to her lips. "Shh. Don't answer me now. We need more time. We need to heal. We need to laugh together and play together and work together. Then, I promise, we'll discuss the future, a future together."

She lifted her lips to his. "I love you, Colby Voss, and—"

Whatever else she was going to say would have to wait for another time because, at that moment, he lowered his lips to hers.

As they kissed, she snuggled into his embrace and Colby realized what the Amish had always known. Simple pleasures were the best. Having Becca, sharing their love, becoming a family someday soon, those were the God-given blessings that would last forever.

EPILOGUE

Four months later

Becca reached for Colby's hand as they walked along the beach. The waves lapped at their feet, and the sun hung low in the evening sky.

"Your family's Virginia Beach home is beautiful, Colby."

Breathing in the salty air, she turned to see their footprints in the sand. Becca remembered a scripture reflection about Jesus carrying a person along the shore during troubled times so that instead of two footprints there was only one.

"I told you my father talked about having to carry such a heavy cross," she said. "As much as he talked about God, he never knew how much he was loved by the Lord. If my *datt* had worried less about himself and more about others, he might have felt his load ease."

Colby squeezed her hand. "You and Katie were a help to him, I know."

"I was too headstrong."

He laughed. "I call that determination, which saved you when you were being held captive by Jacob."

She nodded. "He was a twisted soul who manipulated women for his own desires, including me. But I was young and didn't see who he really was until I took care of his wife."

"At least he lived long enough to confess everything to the sheriff, including that he had started the fire that killed his wife and brother."

"The last I heard," Becca said, "McDougal still claimed he had thought the body recovered from the fire was Jacob's."

Colby nodded. "At least the good folks of Harmony forced the mayor out of office. Tucker sold his real estate holdings and moved north, which left McDougal without a job. His house is in foreclosure, and his trial is still pending for falsifying documents."

"I'm sure justice will be served," Becca said as she sidled closer to Colby. He put his arm around her shoulder as they walked on, both lost in thought.

"My parents like you," Colby finally said.

"Are you sure?"

"Absolutely. They show their love with food. Mom made her special homemade carrot cake for dessert. Dad had the butcher cut extra-thick steaks that he'll grill tonight. You've definitely stolen their hearts."

She laughed. "If we stay too long, I'll gain weight."

"Gloria gave you a thumbs-up."

"She's darling and seems to adore her brother. As do all the girls. I told them they had trained you well since you're such a gentleman."

He playfully splashed water on her legs. "Now you're making fun."

She stopped and looked into his eyes. "Actually I love having a man take care of me."

"You do." He gazed at her, his brown eyes reflecting the love she felt for him.

"Colby, I never thought I'd find a man to love. Not a man who made me feel so special."

"You are special, Becca."

He kissed her long and hard until their toes were buried in the wet sand.

Then turning her around, he pointed to the shoreline.

"Someday, I'd like to have a home on the water. Maybe a beach house."

"You mean after the military?"

He nodded. "Although by that time, the kids will be in college, and I'll need two jobs to foot the bills."

"Maybe your wife will work."

"Whatever she wants to do."

Becca pretended to walk again. "I'm sure you'll be happy."

"Hey." He touched her arm. "Where are you going?"

"Don't you need to find a wife before you plan your future?"

"You're right."

He reached into his pocket and pulled out a small box, his expression suddenly serious. "Becca, would you marry me and be my wife?"

"Oh, Colby." She held out her hand and he slipped the ring on her finger.

She nestled closer, feeling his strong embrace. All the love she had for him welled up within her. She'd found the perfect man, a wonderful, righteous man to walk with her into the future.

"Yes," she said, "I'll be your wife, and we'll have lots of babies, if God wills it, and a house on the beach and a lifetime of love.

Later they drove back to the Voss home. A huge sign hung over the door. "Welcome to the family, Becca! We love you!"

She smiled, wrapping her arm around Colby as they climbed the front steps. After all this time, Becca had a home and a family that cared for her. But more important, she had Colby, the man of her dreams, who would love her and cherish her forever.

Pulling her close, he lowered his lips to hers and kissed her once, twice, three times before he opened the door. She felt a sense of homecoming and knew that the rest of their lives would be as special as today had been with the sunshine and the warm water and blue sky.

With Colby at her side, their life together would be simply wonderful.

* * * * *

Dear Reader

I hope you enjoy *The Agent's Secret Past,* the sixth book in my Military Investigations Series, which features heroes and heroines in the army's Criminal Investigation Division. Each story stands alone so you can read them in any order, either in print or as an ebook: *The Officer's Secret,* book 1; *The Captain's Mission,* book 2; and *The Colonel's Daughter,* book 3; *The General's Secretary,* book 4; and *The Soldier's Sister,* book 5.

In this story, Special Agent Becca Miller must revisit her Amish past in order to solve a murder on post. Teaming up with Special Agent Colby Voss causes problems, both professionally and personally, and forces secrets to be revealed. With nowhere else to turn, they each must turn to God. If you need help, call on the Lord. He will be your shelter in the storm.

I want to hear from you. Email me at debby@debbygiusti.com or write me c/o Love Inspired, 233 Broadway, Suite 1001, New York, NY 10279. Visit my website at www.DebbyGiusti.com and blog with me at www.seekerville.blogspot.com, www.craftieladiesofromance.blogspot.com and www.crossmyheartprayerteam.blogspot.com. As always, I thank God for bringing us together through this story.

Wishing you abundant blessings,

Debby Giusti

Questions for Discussion

1. Compare and contrast the guilt Colby and Becca carried. In either case were their feelings justified? What did they each need to learn?

2. Why did Becca turn away from God? Has there been a time in your life when you've walked away from the Lord? What brought you back?

3. The Amish call themselves plain. Name some of the positive aspects of their way of life. Are there negatives, as well?

4. Where did Becca get her determination and self-sufficiency? Did they serve her well or were they stumbling blocks?

5. Was Colby's protective nature a strength or a weakness? If you asked his sisters, what would they say? What did Colby need to learn?

6. Were there facets of the Amish life that Becca embraced even after she joined the military? Have you ever wanted to simplify your life? What steps would you take to do so?

7. In what ways did Becca see herself in the widow Fannie Lehman?

8. Was Becca able to forgive Jacob? If so, why? Is it easy for you to forgive others or do you hold on to past hurts?

9. How did Jacob's childhood impact his adult life? Did

he love his mother? What did he need to tell her at the end of the story?

10. Who was buried in the Yoder graves? Did Jacob kill his brother? Did he kill his wife? Who set fire to their home?

11. Had you previously heard about Pinecraft? Did it surprise you to learn about the Amish vacation spot? What did Becca see there that touched her heart?

12. Colby grew up in a loving family. Why was he worried about Gloria? How were he and his sister alike?

13. If not for Jacob, do you think Becca would have remained Amish? Was her father a bad man? Did he love his daughters?

14. Becca mentioned both her need to control situations and her own pride. How are pride and control similar?

15. Explain the importance of the treasures Becca kept in her room. What did they symbolize? Did you have a treasure box as a child? Do you remember the mementoes that were special to you?